T0147503

An Unsolved Murder

Murder

An Unsolved Murder

Who can stand against the law of the land?

Anna Bain-Marie

iUniverse, Inc.
Bloomington

An Unsolved Murder
Who can stand against the law of the land?

iUniverse books may be ordered through booksellers or by contacting:

iUniverse
1663 Liberty Drive
Bloomington, IN 47403
www.iuniverse.com
1-800-Authors (1-800-288-4677)

ISBN: 978-1-4620-2719-4 (pbk)
ISBN: 978-1-4620-2720-0 (ebk)

Printed in the United States of America

iUniverse rev. date: 06/16/2011

Contents

Chapter 1

Frosty Bloody Evening

Clementine put the newspaper down on the desk and thoughtfully studied the article she had been reading. The article, buried on page 6 of The Green County Press Gazette, was short and seemingly insignificant. It announced that there had been a meeting of the Green County Airport Commission to determine the feasibility of putting in a longer landing strip to accommodate jet aircraft. The meeting had been held at the Hamburg Hotel on March 20, 1955, beginning at 8:00 p.m.

Clem had left the church choir practice session at 9:00 p.m. or just shortly after, having first put on her red jacket in the coat room. It would have taken her approximately 20 minutes of walking to pass by the Hamburg Hotel and become a witness to the jaw-dropping spectacle that awaited her there.

It was a late winter evening, frosty yet mild, with tiny ice crystals gathering on all exposed surfaces. A halo had formed around each of the street lights. From around the dog-legged corner by the hotel, two tall figures appeared, walking toward her. She tensed slightly, recognizing them immediately. She had known these two brothers since childhood; the taller of the two having taken the title "lord of the underworld" at an early age, and the other professing a keen interest in slashing everything and anyone with his ever-ready switchblade.

A "neighborhood territorial truce" had been reached. They were to have nothing to do with each other, and upon meeting, as they were now, she was to keep her eyes averted, not look at them or speak to them, and they would pass without violence. That was the arrangement. Clem could only hope that the agreement, which had been initiated by Chase, would hold up here on this deserted city sidewalk. Keeping her eyes averted, she bore to the right, and they all passed wordlessly.

But as soon as they had passed each other, Chase, elder brother, stopped and began to speak in low tones to Duke. Clem dared a quick glance back over her left shoulder and saw Duke run across the street into the police station, while Chase stood on the sidewalk looking after him. Clem turned to face whatever lay ahead, wondering what could have triggered such a response from them. Their father had been a policeman, but he had died several years ago.

She rounded the dog-leg corner, keeping a sharp eye out. There was a car idling at the curb in front of the hotel door. A young, blond-haired girl stood leaning against the wall near the far corner of the building. Illuminated by the streetlight, she seemed to be transfixed, staring intently into the vehicle. Clementine couldn't see what the girl was looking at; the rear window of the car was fogged up, making visibility impossible. A trail of dark, viscous-looking fluid ran down the hotel steps from the entrance, went across the sidewalk and disappeared in the shadow behind the car.

What had happened here? What was the substance that ran across the sidewalk? Clem looked intently at the girl as she approached the scene. With an effort, the girl pulled her gaze away from whoever was in the car, jerked her head sideways and looked at Clem, who recognized the girl immediately. The girl was Ida Mae March, and she was no friend of Clementine's. Ida Mae simply rolled on her right shoulder and disappeared around the corner of the building.

Clem stepped across the line of dark fluid that looked suspiciously like blood, and now she drew even with the side window of the idling car. Turning her head to the left, she peered directly into the vehicle. Her jaw dropped as she stopped in her tracks. A man sat behind the steering wheel, clear fluid mingling with blood, all running down across his face. His head was broken! Pieces of skull stuck out here and there above his eyes and ears. His brains bulged out from under a man's dress hat, which looked as if it had been hastily placed on top of the mess that had been his head. His forlorn eyes were still staring at the place where the girl had been standing, as if to say, please don't leave me. He never looked at Clementine. Suddenly, he pulled the gear lever, and the car lurched away, turning left at the intersection.

How was that possible? Clem wondered. He should be dead. Nobody could be alive and have a severe head injury like that, brains sticking out from under his hat. How could he have driven away and even made a left turn at the intersection? Only then did she realize that her mouth was open, and closing it, she turned toward home. When she got to the end of the building, she looked down that street and saw Ida Mae about half a block away.

In the fresh, untrammeled frost covering the sidewalk, Ida Mae's trail was plainly visible. She had been struck with polio in childhood, and it had left her alive but crippled in her left leg. She walked, leaving a drag mark on the frosty sidewalk all the way to where she was making her way towards the town's main street.

Clem slumped against that side of the building, on the corner away from the scene she had witnessed. Peering back around the corner, she tried to observe any detail she might have missed. Now she could see that the trail of blood had run from the hotel entrance, down the steps, across the sidewalk and around the back of the car to the driver's side. There were some signs of people walking in a normal fashion in and out of the hotel in the frost, but near the corner, the frosty sidewalk was well-trodden around where Ida Mae had been standing. Clem knew these people and she knew what they had been doing, up against the wall.

Sighing deeply, she turned to leave, jumping into the air, she was so startled. Ida Mae was right behind her, and Ida Mae now laughed at her, a derisive, unpleasant laugh.

"I had to come back and make sure it was you," Ida Mae said, narrowing her eyes.

Clem's only response, after muttering a few swear words under her breath, was her usual admonition to Ida Mae, said as meanly as possible.

"Stay the hell away from me, Ida Mae! I mean it!" Clem turned and walked away toward home, leaving Ida Mae to resume whatever activities she had planned for the evening. As Clem walked, a dog began to bark, from somewhere off to the right. A forlorn bark, deep-voiced and steady as a drumbeat; she wondered if the dog was aware of the man's plight by sheer animal instinct. From the direction of the hospital came the sound of a car horn, blowing steadily. She knew the man had fallen across the steering wheel, onto his car horn, trying to drive himself to the hospital. She felt certain that he was dead.

Chapter 2

Police Theory

As Clem folded the newspaper and placed it back on her father's desk, he entered the room and looked sharply at her.

"The police are coming here," he said, "to ask you some questions about the other night. What happened? Why didn't you say anything?"

Clementine shrugged. "For one thing, I don't think I've seen you for more than a minute. I didn't actually see anything happening. What I saw was some people leaving the scene. I don't really know what happened there."

She turned to face him, biting her lip. "I saw someone who looked very familiar, somehow, but his head was broken open, and his brains were falling out."

Her father stared at her, nodding slowly. "It was Eric Alderson. He's not dead, at least not yet. They've flown him to another hospital. They think he was attacked and bludgeoned on the street, outside the Hamburg Hotel."

Clem was startled. "That's not so. I saw a trail of blood coming out of the hotel. He was attacked inside, not on the street. Any investigation would plainly see that."

Her father shrugged and shook his head. "Tell it to the cops." He riffled through the papers on his desk. "I've got an appointment to go to. Can you handle this by yourself?"

Clem nodded, and soon her father had left the house. He was an insurance salesman, working from an office in his home. His hours were anytime someone called him, and he was always on the go. Clem acted as a sometime secretary for him, answering the phone as he wanted her to, sorting through and organizing papers on his desk, and filing in a very large, antique filing cabinet. In fact, all the furniture in his office was ponderous and antique, except for his desk, which was boringly functional.

Clem's mother, Phyllis, whose health had always been fragile, was currently in the hospital with yet another round of ailments. Her maternal grandmother, Maria, lived with the family, helped with household chores, and also cared for her daughter, Phyllis.

Clementine was a high school student and tried to help out at home as much as possible. She had red hair, green eyes and a creamy white complexion splashed with freckles across her nose. She wished she had black hair, brown eyes and an olive complexion, like her father; she wore her hair long and straight, in what she hoped was a "Cleopatra-like" style. And, of course, everyone called her "Clem."

Since the events of Wednesday night, things had been quiet. At school, she did not see Ida Mae anywhere, but that was not unusual. They had no classes together and avoided each other as much as possible. She knew that at least three people had seen her as she walked by the hotel; Chase, Duke and Ida Mae. She knew that Chase had sent Duke into the police station, probably to report the bludgeoning, but why then would they think the attack had occurred on the street? Of course, that was probably just a wild rumor.

And then there was Eric Alderson, the victim of the attack. No wonder he looked familiar. He belonged to the same church. His father had been at the choir practice also. The Aldersons were the church's most prominent family, extremely wealthy and influential, and Clem had often seen Eric and spoken to him. Even his car now fell into place in her mind, for she had seen it in the church parking lot many times.

Now, she thought it likely that Eric had attended the meeting of the Green County Airport Commission to discuss the extended runway proposition. That should be easy to verify. Was Eric attacked at, before, or during the meeting? Certainly, if she was an investigator, she would be talking to the people at that meeting, and trying to find out who was in the hotel at that time. It was likely that the attack occurred very close to the time that she was walking towards the hotel. Burning with curiosity and eager to be helpful, she paced back and forth in the foyer, checking continually for the arrival of the police.

And they did come, about 4:00 that afternoon. Clem was tense, curious, and glad she didn't have to wait any longer. There were three men; a sergeant, who drove the squad, a plain-clothes detective, and even the chief of police, Jack Mooney. The sergeant remained in the squad car at the curb. Chief Mooney walked into the living room off the foyer and seated himself without a word. From there, he could hear both the questions and the responses without being right in the room. After a few preliminaries, the investigator asked Clem to give an account of where she had been that evening, what she had been doing, the times of each occurrence, and especially, what she had witnessed. Clem gave as complete a description of everything as she was able. It seemed to her that she talked a very long time.

When she was finished, she felt relieved. She had done a good thing, doing her civic duty by cooperating with the police, being as helpful as possible. She was not prepared for what followed. The investigator smiled.

"You're lying!" he announced with conviction, slapping his notebook closed.

Clem was so startled, that she could think of nothing to say in reply. She simply stared, wide-eyed, at the officer. After a few moments of supreme confusion on her part, she finally managed to ask, "Well then, just what do you think happened?"

"You were there on the street that evening. You tell me!"

"I've already told you everything I did and saw."

After this exchange went on for a while, it became obvious to Clem that the investigating officer wanted her to say that she was there on the street all along, not at church choir practice, and that the only thing that remained unclear in the officer's mind, was just what her involvement had been in the attack on Eric Alderson, who had happened to be walking by.

Clem was astounded. "What about the trail of blood coming out of the hotel?" she queried. By now, the police chief had walked into the foyer and was watching the two of them closely. The two men looked at each other knowingly.

"What trail of blood? There was no trail of blood."

Another half hour of wrangling over everything Clem had testified to passed, with Clem getting very stubborn and refusing to testify to anything other than what she had already stated. There were some threats made about her testimony being used against her in a court of law, but Clem folded her arms across her chest and stuck out her lower lip.

When the men saw that she was not going to budge, they called it off. The investigator left, but Chief Mooney turned as he was going out the door.

"If anything ever happens to that poor girl as a result of your lies," he intoned darkly, "I'm going to hold you personally responsible!"

As if a clarion call had sounded, Clem realized, in that moment, that something *was* going to happen to someone. But he could only be speaking about Ida Mae, right?

Chapter 3

The Frontier Forest

The March family, like so many other pioneers, went as far upstream as they could on their makeshift raft, bringing all their earthly possessions with them, including a rooster and several hens. They were stopped, as others had been stopped before them, by a rapids in the river that they could not overcome by pulling the raft through, using ropes along the bank. There was already a tavern on the bank of the river where other families had been stopped by the same circumstances. But the town they were traveling to lay farther upstream, and after spending a few days resting from their journey, they pushed on by land on a crude road that already existed, having converted their raft into a cart with home-made wheels. That small town was Greenwood, the center of Green County, with a thriving, boom-town economy that the March family hoped to get in on.

Before long, Grandfather March and his son, Calvin, were hired by the railroad. Tracks were needed, in order to transport by rail, all the materials that came and went through the seemingly endless forests and rivers of a vast and bounteous land. Timber was the primary export, while all things domestic, and all manner of machinery and equipment came back to town from the outside world.

But life was full of hardships for the railroad workers, and grandfather died of pneumonia in the hard winter of 1932. Calvin suffered a terrible injury at work, losing his right arm. Little Ida Mae was born to Calvin and Lucy March in 1938. But Lucy died soon after, and Calvin died in 1942, when Ida Mae was only four years old. Only her grandmother Gladys remained alive, and her eyesight was rapidly failing. Gladys received a small pension from the railroad of $15.00 per month. They lived upstairs in a tall, narrow, clapboard house across the street from a small grocery. Insulation, in those days, was rarely used in home construction. The most they had against the cold winds and winter frost were pieces of cardboard tacked up where air was rushing through.

Ida Mae was always hungry and would cross the street to the grocery, even when just a small child, so she could hang out around the back door and beg for handouts from the grocer, Mr. Tillerman. Not an unkind man, he sometimes gave her whatever he could spare. She would take the food she got home to her granny and share it with the old, blind woman. If it was spoiling vegetables, they could be trimmed and cooked with fair results. Ida Mae soon became her grandmother's main support in life, buying what she needed and bringing everything to her. She quickly learned the value of each piece of money, was there at granny's side for every bill-paying. She made sure that Gladys wasn't being cheated and was her constant companion. Ida Mae had an older brother, much older, but no one knew what happened to him, whether he was dead or alive. He had disappeared one day back in the city that they came from and was never seen again.

Chapter 4

Another Killer Strikes

Ida Mae developed strategies for living on the streets at an early age, doing anything she could for money, food, or to gain influence with people who were well-to-do. She suffered from malnutrition, had a perennial infection of her eyes, making them sore and crusty, and was seldom clean or well-clothed. Later, she learned that these attributes, the obvious result of extreme poverty, could be a meal ticket in itself and used her appearance to wheedle as much as she could from sympathetic onlookers. But it wasn't enough in the summer of 1944, when she was 6 years old.

Polio was still a terrible force to be reckoned with that year, just before Dr. Jonas Salk et al. brought their vaccine to bear on it and eliminated it for the rest of the century, at least. One day, Gladys just couldn't stay upstairs any longer, not knowing where Ida Mae had gone. She made it down the stairs and across the street to the grocery store. Mr. Tillerman called the police so Gladys could report Ida Mae missing. Lieutenant Jack Mooney, not yet the chief of police, answered the call.

He knew about Gladys and Ida Mae, living alone in the unheated upstairs two rooms of the house across from Tillerman's Grocery, but he had not, nor had anyone else, intervened in their living arrangements, even though they showed extreme poverty. Many people in those days, and in that town, were terribly poor. Listening to the old woman's story that Ida Mae had not come home, but that some animal had crawled in and was hiding behind the couch, making frightening noises, he decided to accompany her across the street to find out what was going on upstairs.

Taking Gladys by the arm, he helped her back across the street and up the stairs to her rooms. Pulling the battered couch away from the wall, he found little Ida Mae curled up in the fetal position, having difficulty breathing, tongue swollen, eyes glazed with fever, the stench of sickness and death coming from her. An ambulance took Ida Mae to the hospital; Mooney did not think she would live. Tears came to his eyes as he contemplated how cruel her life must have been.

But Ida Mae did survive, and when she returned to her grandmother, Lieutenant Mooney was amazed by the change in her. The hospital personnel had bathed her, gotten rid of head lice, crusty eyes, malnutrition and dirty clothes. Her naturally curly hair gleamed like gold in the sun. She had survived the polio, but would have a limp for the rest of her life. He left leg was stiff, paralyzed.

Another change came for Ida Mae. Jack Mooney took a personal interest in her life. The County Welfare Department was called in, and Ida Mae became a ward of the Court. This provided a little more money for her and Gladys to live on, another $10.00 per month. But Mooney's interest in Ida Mae was to have her become a prostitute as soon as possible. He told her that was where the real money lay, and that he would see to it that she was not harmed by any of the customers she took on. Or if anyone, for that matter, ever sought to harm her, they would answer to him. She didn't have to rush into this. No, better to take her time and think about it for awhile; give her a couple of years. She was still pretty young for that kind of life. In fact, Mooney assured his young protégé, he would personally come and pick her up and bring her back home from her jobs, just to make sure she was being treated right, until she was "established." Ida Mae's eyes were wide with wonder at all this, but she felt certain that she had been rescued from a hellish life by Lieutenant Mooney. She had already heard some things on the street and was wise to what he was telling her, or so she thought. He even gave her a little whistle and hung it around her neck.

"If anyone tries to hurt you, or you need help anytime, just blow this whistle. I'll tell the other men on the force to listen for that whistle. Someone will come right away." She nodded, wordless with wonder.

"Oh, and one other thing, Ida Mae," he said, smiling and looking into her eyes, "all this is just between you and me. Nobody else needs to know a thing, not even your granny. Got it? I may have other little jobs you can do for me. There might even be something extra in it for you."

Chapter 5

Mooney's Law of the Land

Jack Mooney grew up in and around Greenwood; his father was one of the first settlers to arrive in the untamed frontier town. The senior Mooneys had 12 children and liked to brag that they were related to just about everyone in town. Mrs. Mooney was French and Indian, and married Jack's father right after he arrived. There were 8 sons and 4 daughters, all of whom grew up and had large families of their own.

At an early age, Jack knew he was meant to take charge of the people who lived here. He quickly learned to dominate his brothers and sisters. He knew every single person who lived in town, where they lived, and later, what their strengths and weaknesses were. He studied every detail of peoples' lives, even down to who had telephones and who did not. It was their weaknesses that both fascinated and repelled him. At an early age, he found that helping to make moonshine in the swamps with some interesting fellows from the big city could also produce an income that raised his status considerably amongst his peers.

Early on, he formed a gang that dominated the streets of town, taking advantage wherever they could of those weaknesses that Jack had noticed; everything from selling phony baseball cards to turning girlfriends out as prostitutes; from procuring moonshine for taverns to robbing and beating men who had won other men's money gambling. Jack was on top of everything "interesting" that happened in the town. It came as something of a joke, at least at first, when he went into the field of law enforcement and began to legitimize his activities. For as many of his gang members who were so disposed, he put in a good word for them, and soon they also found themselves being hired as policemen.

He made friends with other people in top positions. The Green County judge, for instance, became a close confidante. Judge Carmine Williams was sleek, polished and determined to have it his way. His attitude towards malefactors and women was patronizing, unless the public eye was upon him, in which case he handed out harsh sentences to men and became even more patronizing towards women. He had a taste for corruption that made Jack Mooney smile knowingly.

Both men were possessed of good looks and deep, manly voices that made anything they said sound like Biblical pronouncements that were not to be argued with. Judge Williams was blonde; his rapidly balding pate still held remnants of flaxen hair. His sharp blue eyes peered out from behind gleaming, gold-rimmed glasses. His appearance bespoke polished refinement, and he lived sensibly. His house on Knob Hill was still the biggest in town, but he did not flaunt his wealth before the residents. He was a member of the country club and enjoyed his golf outings as often as he could.

Jack, who was dark-haired with brown eyes and a manly physique, did not belong to the country club and shunned all outward appearance of unjustified easy living. And he didn't live easy, kept going until all hours and demanded that anyone working with him put in as many hours as he did. If they failed him, he was sure to make a note of it. He quickly rose in the police force, soon enough becoming the Chief of Police.

He ate at a neighborhood restaurant where his wife did the cooking, and soon his sons and daughters were helping in the restaurant, too. Eventually Jack bought the place and made sure that anyone entering was a family friend or confidante. No one dared enter this family enclave without his say-so.

His house was right next door to the restaurant, which was perched on a small hill just outside the town, and right behind the restaurant was a gully. The gully hosted a stream that fed into a larger river that ran through town. Whenever they had trash at the place, they simply threw it out the back door and pushed it downhill. Eventually, stuff made its way down to the stream and at least some of it got carried off to the river, but the majority of garbage and refuse simply littered the hillside behind the restaurant and became known, locally, as Diners Dump. In an age when everyone seemed to think that rivers and streams were meant to be filled with refuse and offal, this wouldn't have been remarkable. Except that twice, a body was found mired, mutilated and eaten away, at the mouth of the stream and sometimes, a smell so horrid would emanate from Diners Dump that people would suggest to each other that the smell was caused by another body being thrown out the back door of the restaurant. Most people just laughed, but it did cause some prickly sensations at the back of the neck. Handily enough, a cemetery lay just across the road from Mooney's place, and eventually the remains of those two individuals, identified only by who had been missing for some time, found their way into it. As far as what had happened to those men, no one seemed to know, and no one came forward to speak up about the matter.

Judge Williams and Chief Mooney quickly formed an easy-going alliance. The judge was certain that he was Mooney's boss, but Mooney, while not contesting the matter, was equally certain that the judge was in his pocket. They did not give the appearance of being fast friends; each man kept to his own social circle, but all their activities dovetailed nicely. Mostly, their fledgling syndicate ran drugs and prostitution in the county.

Not many people were in need of hard drugs in those days, but those who required them quickly learned the drill, at Mooney's direction. He had no objection to people taking drugs. That was their business, as long as they did it his way. A drug dealer from the big city was allowed to enter the county but not come into the city limits of Greenwood. The dealer had to wait at a highway intersection in a wooded copse on Tuesday nights, beginning at 8:00 p.m. every fortnight. Those who wanted to buy had to get themselves out to that intersection, and by flashlight, signal their arrival to the dealer, who would then approach and sell them hard core stuff, like heroine or cocaine. Marijuana could be purchased also, very quietly, but that drug was funneled to the customers from another source, mostly. That source was controlled exclusively by Mooney and his gang. Mooney knew the identities of each and every drug user, and often stood in the woods nearby watching and listening to the proceedings. The drug users even banded together and often came in small groups, because frankly, they were afraid of the wooded darkness that surrounded these transactions.

Prostitution had been rampant during the logging days of the forests and settlement of Greenwood, and it wasn't much different now. Since childhood, Mooney had been active in selecting young girls to take up the oldest profession, and it was never too soon, as far as he was concerned. The girls he preyed upon were either orphans or had suffered some serious social downfall that rendered them more likely to be pushed into the trade. He thought that all women were whores, only differing in size, age and a few physical details. Some whores were only barflies and often got beat up for their troubles. Mooney even thought that his protection for certain females in town was beneficent. Without his tolerance and good will, what chance did they have? In his own mind, he was the good guy, keeping law and order.

His idea was that there were two laws. One law was Judge Williams' law, made up by a bunch of meddling, interfering men who lived in big cities and didn't understand the realities of life that he had observed since childhood. The other law was his law, the law as he saw it. That was the real law of the land. Anyone who didn't see things his way was an enemy. As long as the judge's rulings coincided with his and didn't interfere with his own aims, the "other" law could proceed with all due respect. In a difference of opinion, Mooney would quietly back off and wait for the ball to come into his court again. He would never jeopardize his position of power by an outright confrontation against the written law. Outwardly, he appeared to be a bastion of propriety. But could anyone really stand up against Mooney's law?

Chapter 6

Closing In

Clementine and her grandmother, Maria, were waiting anxiously late Tuesday afternoon when Herman brought Phyllis home from the hospital. They expected that mom would want to go right to bed and recuperate, but she walked into the kitchen and sat down, resting one arm casually on the table. Only the look on her pale face and in her steely gray eyes gave away that she was on the warpath. Herman, Clem's father, looked on quietly from his office, adjacent to the kitchen.

"I want answers," she began, looking directly at Clem. "Were you, or were you not, at choir practice on Wednesday night?"

Clem nodded, seating herself across from her mother. "Yes, I was, until 9:00, as usual. Then I walked home."

"That's not what we've heard," said Phyllis. "We've heard that you never went to choir practice, you were hanging out with a couple of young men around the Hamburg Hotel."

Clem shook her head vigorously. "No, that's not right. You can ask the pastor . . . ask anyone who was at choir practice."

Phyllis and Herman exchanged looks. "We've asked the pastor, and he said that you weren't there."

"Impossible!" cried Clem, then quickly calmed herself down. It was a frequent cross-examination tactic her mother had used since early childhood, designed to scare "the truth" out of her. She shook her head and looked imploringly at her father, sighing deeply. But he had never interfered with his wife's tactics and did not do so now. Eventually, the questioning ended with nothing resolved, mother apparently not believing anything she said, and Clem in tears, hating both her parents for never, ever supporting her.

Later that evening, as Clem made her way to the shower, she overheard her mother saying to her father, "Well, you can't fight City Hall!" in a resigned tone. *So you'd rather believe I was on the street*, Clem thought gloomily, *doing it with those guys?*

"Where do you think you're going?" demanded Phyllis, as Clem took hold of the doorknob the next evening at 7:30 p.m.

"Choir practice, as usual. It's Wednesday," not turning to face her mother. There was no response, so Clem opened the door and left the house.

Choir practice did not seem any different than any other Wednesday evening. At 9:00, they disbanded, and while getting her jacket from the rack, Clem turned to see the pastor standing nearby and asked, "Pastor, you know I was at choir practice last Wednesday, don't you? Could you do me a favor? Could you please go to the police station and make a signed statement to that effect? That I was here at choir practice last Wednesday evening?"

Pastor Beyer exploded. "No, I will not get involved in your civil troubles! I'll tell you the same thing I've already told the police! I don't want to get involved. Your father has already asked me the same thing. No! I won't get involved."

The other choir members hurried away, apparently deaf and dumb to what they must have overheard. But one man remained standing in the background, looking on. It was Eric's father, Charles Alderson, whose son was so brutally attacked last Wednesday evening. Eric's father, who knew perfectly well that Clementine had been at choir practice then.

It was he who did go to the police station the next day to make out an affidavit regarding his and Clem's presence at choir practice on the night in question. This should end the controversy for once and for all, he thought, as he put on his hat and started for the door. Behind him, he heard the sound of paper tearing gently. He turned and saw the desk sergeant, leering at him now, slowly tearing the affidavit into small pieces. He watched, glaring, as the sergeant delicately moved his hand over the waste basket beside his desk, and foppishly, with an exaggerated swirl of his hand, let the pieces flutter into the basket.

Alderson adjusted his hat and left the building. Wealth, power and position, truth or goodness meant nothing to these rascals, headed by their power-mad chief of police. It was, for them, a reason to hate those who had such attributes. Charles knew all about it.

The chief of police was not the only one who wanted power; it was Eric who had attended the County Commission meeting, at which he threatened to do everything in his power to prevent the advent of jet plane traffic into their small town. He was speaking, of course, for his father. Charles owned and controlled the town's main business venture, Alderson Enterprises, and he did not want to lose control of the airport, which he himself had built for his company's interests. Once you let jet aircraft land here, he thought, I'll be pushed aside, forgotten, and other business interests would be sure to follow. He hated being the biggest property taxpayer in town, but it made him feel justified in controlling and even stopping other business interests from entering "his" domain.

Of course, someone at the meeting had objected to Eric's hard-line, hard-nosed approach, and he could almost guess who had attacked his son. Filing a police report about the attack had been galling. They had treated the whole incident with cavalier indifference, suggesting that Eric had said or done something to provoke, and thereby, justify the attack.

At least he could talk to Clementine's father and mother, let them know that their daughter had not, could not possibly have been involved in the attack on his son, or in any of the salacious activities that he guessed had occurred outside of the hotel. He would try to help this girl, if possible, regain her good standing in the community and with her own parents, who didn't seem to know who was lying and who was telling the truth. Charles shook his head in disbelief at that.

He said a silent prayer of gratitude that Eric had survived this dreadful ordeal. He had, in fact, been pronounced dead on arrival at the hospital, when he had been brought inside from his car. But he had surprised everyone, returned from the dead and, miraculously, was mending, at least physically. Though his mind was . . . . well, it would take time, but the best psychologists and doctors and hospitals would do everything humanly possible to bring Eric back to normal. The Aldersons would spend any amount of money to make sure that their son recovered, became himself again.

Chapter 7

The Protégé

The first time Mooney drove Ida Mae to a "job" he had lined up for her, he was more nervous than she was, and she sensed his uneasiness right away. This made her all the more determined to be stoical, no matter what happened. She was a young girl who seemed much younger than she was to Mooney, probably because she was small, or perhaps stunted, for her age.

He had made all the arrangements through one of his plain-clothes detectives. The customer was a traveling salesman, staying in a downtown hotel above a bar. He came to town regularly, and Mooney made sure to get as much information about the customer as he needed to be certain of his good behavior, just in case Ida Mae got hurt or cheated. Mooney wanted to make sure no one would get away with anything. The customer wanted "young stuff, not used up."

The detective was waiting in the cramped entryway that served both the bar and the hotel.

He had his back to the bar door and ushered Ida Mae to the stairs, told her it was the second door on the left.

"You know your left from your right, don't you?" he asked, grinning. Ida Mae stuck out her left hand in silence. He guffawed, nodded and closed the door behind her as she made her way up the stairs.

Waiting outside in the car, Mooney was apprehensive. She was a cripple, so young. If anything went wrong, it wouldn't be good for himself or her, either. The detective joined him in the car. It was a wintry night, and their breathing soon had the windows steamed up. Mooney turned on the windshield wipers, as if that would clear up the inside condensation. Detective Jones looked at him thoughtfully. "Let's drive around the block a few times," he suggested. "You can turn on the blower."

"I can turn on the blower any time I want to!" snapped Mooney, but he drove around for awhile while the windshield cleared up. Back at the hotel, he told Jones to go upstairs and make sure Ida Mae got down the stairs without falling. "Poor thing," he muttered to himself. "It's rough, all right, the first time and all, what with that bad leg."

When Ida Mae got back in the car, Mooney drove her back to her grandmother's house, marveling at her deadpan expression. He shook his head in admiration. "What a tough little nut!" he said, under his breath.

"All right?" he asked, when he stopped the car in front of her house. He leaned forward to be able to see as much of her face as he could. She looked at him and nodded, making her face as hard as possible.

"You got your money from Jones, right?" Another quick nod and almost a smile. Jack let out a sigh of relief. "You go in now, do whatever you have to do, get cleaned up, get some rest. Okay? Okay. We'll talk tomorrow."

Upstairs, sitting on the battered couch that was her bed, she laid out the money she had earned for what she had done. It was a curious mixture of feelings that swept through her; she shuddered once, but looked steadfastly at the money lying beside her. She kept repeating over and over to herself that it was her money, she had earned it, had earned the right to keep it; that money was power and that she had stepped into good fortune in her life. Powerful people surrounded her now, people who had her interests at heart and would protect her, as long as she was willing to do whatever they asked of her. Could she do this again? Sure . . . . sure she could.

In the years that followed, Mooney was puzzled by only one thing; that no matter how much money Ida Mae made, her appearance never changed very much. She had been downright lovely to look at when she had gotten out of the hospital. But by then, she had already learned her sure-fire ways of getting sympathy and cooperation from others. She had learned that her crusty eyes, dirty yellow hair and sour smell of privation were no deterrent to men who wanted her. In fact, there were some men who absolutely needed that. It gave them a sense of power and superiority over someone so lowly. Jack guessed that by now, he must have seen just about everything in what men wanted in their whores.

A couple of years later, when Ida Mae's grandmother, Gladys, fell and broke her wrist, Ida Mae paid for all the medical bills with cash. Mooney was so proud. Ida Mae was his protégé, his best student. She listened to every word he said, took it all to heart and made it her credo.

She readily formed a gang of her own, and there was no disputing who the boss was. Just how she managed to gain control of a six foot tall, gangly teenage boy puzzled Mooney at first, but he laughed when he realized just how she gathered her disciples. She found things out about people, things they didn't want made public, then sympathized, growled and threatened them with exposure. She flaunted her relationship with the police chief in front of them, then offered them amnesty, even her own protection. Soon she had them cooperating in little plots to entrap other unfortunate children into her gang. They had to do whatever she told them to do or bear the consequences. All these children suffered from some sort of unfortunate circumstance in their lives, and they were willing to do anything to get her protection from the law, and her silence. In a few years, little Ida Mae, an impoverished cripple, had money stashed somewhere safe and a gang of about 12 children of varying ages and circumstances, waiting every day to do her bidding.

Chapter 8

My New Best Friend

They were all in 5th grade together; Ida Mae, Clementine and Sylvia, Judge Williams' daughter. Ida Mae, who'd been held back a year, was one year older than her classmates, due to the polio she had suffered. It was then, when Sylvia was 10 years old, that her father, the judge, began to molest her. Mrs. Williams had recently made a decision that she no longer wanted to have intercourse, wanted her life to be free of all that "disgusting business." The judge then turned to his daughter.

But Sylvia, red-haired, freckle-faced and feisty, could not be quiet about it, as "good girls" should. Soon she burst forth at school, during class, in a tirade of screaming, crying and begging for help. All eyes in the classroom turned towards her, and the teacher came to her side to try to console her and to find out exactly what had happened to her. Sylvia did not quiet down, pounded on her desk, and within minutes she had loudly blubbered out what was happening to her at home. The teacher hastened to quiet her, kept saying "shush, shush." Sylvia finally quieted, sobbing gently into her folded arm, head on her desk.

A couple of days later, she again erupted into a screaming, crying tirade against her father. This time, the teacher left and brought back the principal to hear the girl out. All the principal could do was keep repeating "shush, shush" with arms folded, while the teacher patted Sylvia's shoulder. Clem watched, along with all the other children, and thought that the judge was surely in a lot of trouble, and deserved whatever punishment society would dish out to a man who ruined his own daughter. Just what Ida Mae was thinking was nobody's business but hers.

The tirades did not cease, and eventually the Superintendent of Schools was called in to hear and see for himself what all the fuss was about. After hearing the sobbing girl, seated at her desk, the superintendent drew a long breath and addressed the entire class. His speech was flowery and full of phrases that sounded like he meant business, but the gist of it, as far as Clem could understand it, was that the children should just "get on with your lives now."

When he left the room, one of the boys took out a small notebook from his shirt pocket and began to write. Eddie always wrote things down that happened in or out of school. There was a dead silence for some time; then Sylvia's best friend, Joan, came to her side, snuggled into the seat with her, and began to whisper in her ear. Class resumed as before.

Shortly, Clem dared to look back at Sylvia, wondering how she was faring. To her consternation, both Sylvia and Joan were looking directly at her, and Joan had an evil look in her eyes. Sylvia was nodding slowly.

After school let out for the day, Clem started for home, but Sylvia was waiting for her, while Joan stood far behind, watching. "Guess what?" exclaimed Sylvia, enthusiastically,

"You're my best friend, now! You should come over to my house with me and stay overnight!"

Clem's reaction was immediate. "No!" she shouted. "I won't do it!" She understood what was going on here. She had red hair and a few freckles, she was the same age as Sylvia. Joan had come up with a plan to try to substitute Clem for Sylvia and thus end the misery that Sylvia was going through. It had become obvious that no adults had the courage to face up to the judge. Clem stamped her foot to enforce her refusal and turned to walk away.

"Of course you'll do it!" Sylvia chimed after her and meaningfully added, "My mother will call your mother!" Clem hurried away.

When she arrived home, her mother was just finishing a most pleasant conversation with someone who had obvious clout. Hanging up the phone, she turned to Clem and told her that, tomorrow night, she'd be spending the night at Sylvia's house. The judge's wife had personally invited her. Clem said nothing, not knowing how to broach this taboo subject or even how to explain what she thought was going on.

Next day, after school let out, Clem ascended the hill with Sylvia, while Joan was nowhere to be seen. Eddie took his notebook out of his shirt pocket and scribbled in it, looking after the girls.

The house on "knob hill" as it was called by the local residents was old; one of the first and biggest houses built in Greenwood, but also one of the most elaborate, sporting an attached gazebo and even a turret. Sylvia's mother, Carol, was waiting in the kitchen. As soon as the girls were seated at the table, she sat down and engaged both of them in polite conversation, at first. Then, looking directly into Clem's eyes, she pointedly asked, "What do you want?" Clem understood immediately that the mother knew all about her daughter's situation, having helped to create it, and was already on board with the plan to substitute Clementine for Sylvia.

"A bath! And a shampoo! And I want all my clothes washed, dried and ironed before school tomorrow!" Clem cheerfully, innocently crowed.

Carol and Sylvia looked at each other, the mother with a questioning look, while Sylvia shook her head and raised her shoulders slightly. Apparently, some things had not been brought up to Clem, as had been planned. Perhaps there had been no time, during school hours.

"All right," said Carol sagely, "A bath, shampoo, and clean clothes. I think we can do that for you."

It wasn't that Clem was too dim-witted to ask for something of value for the intended service to be rendered. Though she could not bring herself to confide in her mother, she had no intention; no, not for a million dollars, not for all the tea in China, would she agree to any kind of "deal" to allow some old guy to mess with her! She had deliberately asked only for what she would have gotten at home of an evening, what could normally be expected for any girl to have in order to get ready for bedtime. She had already given her refusal yesterday, had hoped and prayed that she would be saved from such foul use.

Later, after Clem had received such care as she had asked for; when the girls were sitting at the kitchen table doing their homework and Carol was cooking supper, the judge came home. If he knew about the arrangement, he said nothing, did not poke his head into the kitchen. He sat in a very large chair in the living room, reading his evening paper, silent and distant. Carol sent Clem into the living room to place a bowl of flowers on a table there, and she had to walk right by the judge's chair. She knew he was watching her as she walked by. She thought "the beast" would not appear to be watching her on the return, and indeed, his head was deep in the newspaper on her way back to the kitchen.

For being her "new best friend," Clem noted that Sylvia barely spoke to her. After a cold and pretentious supper, Sylvia and Clem changed into pajamas, ready for bed. The bedroom was narrow, painted yellow, and contained two twin beds along one wall. Clem had expected something more luxurious for this mansion on the hill, but the old house was just that, after all, an old house.

The girls settled into their respective beds, the light was turned off, and mother left the room, closing the door. It was very dark and quiet. Sylvia did not say a word. In the darkness, Clem began her preparations to avoid the beast. Scrunching herself close to the wall under the bedding, she pulled the covers back as if someone had left the bed. She rumpled the covers up towards the wall where she was hiding, then slipped herself over the edge of the bed into the space between the bed and the wall. Her slim hand came out and made the final adjustments to pillow and covers to be sure she was completely out of sight. As far as she was concerned, if she had to hang there by her toenails and fingernails all night long, she would. She felt strong and wide awake.

It wasn't really that long to wait. Sylvia's breathing had become gentle and slowed, when Clem heard the bedroom door open quietly. Soft footsteps tentatively approached her bed. Soon, a hand caressed the spot where a person should have been sleeping. Clem held her breath and waited. The footsteps slipped away, towards the other bed. Clem waited. Sylvia began to sob, at first gently, then she wailed loudly. Clem immediately lifted herself back onto the bed and put the covers over herself. In the hallway beyond, a light snapped on, and the doorway was flung open. Carol snapped on the bedroom light, and Clem winced and shut her eyes tightly.

"What's going on in here?" demanded Carol. Clem saw the judge, bent over Sylvia's bed, just straightening up.

"Sylvia's had one of her bad dreams again," explained the judge, but both he and Carol were looking hard at Clem. "Where were you?" he asked. "You weren't there just a minute ago."

"I went to the bathroom," Clem lied sleepily, rubbing her eyes. Carol whirled around and disappeared down the hallway. Clem knew she was surely caught in her lie, but what else could she have said? And they didn't say anything to her, just exchanged looks when Carol returned. Sylvia's sobbing had subsided into sniffles. The light was turned off, the door was shut, and Clem and Sylvia went to sleep then for the rest of the night, undisturbed.

At breakfast, there were only the two girls at the table, eating cold toast and juice. Sylvia was not in a good mood. She told Clem that she was no longer her friend, and that she would not be invited back, ever. That was just fine, Clem thought, but she still felt badly for Sylvia and her problem, which was not to be wished on anyone. They put on their coats and went to school, Sylvia stomping ahead angrily.

As the day progressed, Clem felt happier and happier, as if a great burden had been lifted from her. She felt she had done it, had come through a difficult passage, had not been harmed, her principles had not been compromised. She said a prayer of thanks. During afternoon recess, she was standing alone when Ida Mae came up behind her and began to speak. Clem jumped, startled.

"Of all the stupid things to do!" growled Ida Mae softly. "Some people just don't know when they've got it made! You'd give up all that and ask for a bath?" For once, Clem had nothing to say in return. It was obvious Ida Mae and everyone else knew all about it. To her surprise, it was Ida Mae who went up the hill with Sylvia after school, Eddie duly noting it in his little notebook. Clem turned and walked home, feeling very good indeed.

Just as she entered the house, the phone was ringing. There was no one home to answer it, and she rushed in, leaving the door wide open. "Hello?" she asked breathlessly.

"I know where you live, and I can reach out any time I want to, and get you!" said a deep, snarling voice into her ear. "So you had better watch your step!" Then click, and the line went dead. She recognized the judge's voice immediately. "I can do that!" she said, brightly, hopefully, to no one there.

Chapter 9

Clem's Perspective

"Come here, Clem dear," said Phyllis, patting the couch next to her. It was Sunday afternoon, after church, to which Herman had stopped going regularly, years ago. He was now a Christmas-Easter kind of guy, but Phyllis made an effort to attend more frequently. She had gone to church today because she felt so much better, and she did want to see and hear Clem singing with the choir. Clem joined her on the couch, and Phyllis hugged her. Clem hugged her mother back, while Herman watched over the top of his Sunday newspaper, his eyes glowing with happiness.

"I'm sorry if we seemed not to believe you," began Phyllis. "I know you were right where you were supposed to be that night. Charles Alderson stopped to talk to me after church today and told me all about it. He also told me something else. He told me that he had gone to the police station to make out an affidavit that you were at choir practice that evening, but that they refused to accept the affidavit."

Clem looked worried. "Why would the police not accept it?"

"I don't know, honey," said Phyllis sadly. "But I can tell you that the Chief of Police, Jack Mooney, came to see me in the hospital, just before I came home, and he's the one who told me you had not gone to choir practice. He's the one who insists that you were loitering on the street that night with those two boys."

Clem stared into her mother's eyes. "Why would the police deliberately lie, sneak around behind my back, even bother my mother in the hospital, to . . ." Then she remembered the stern warning that Jack Mooney delivered to her as he left the house. His words came back to her now. "If anything ever happens to that poor girl as a result of your lies, I'm going to hold you personally responsible." Clem could only shake her head and wonder. Why would anything happen to Ida Mae? He had been talking about Ida Mae, hadn't he?

Later that afternoon, resting and dozing off in her bedroom, Clem thought back on everything that had ever happened between herself and Ida Mae. Ever since Herman Hammond had moved his wife and daughter to Greenwood to open the insurance agency for the company he worked for, there had been a problem with Ida Mae. Though Ida Mae lived at least six blocks away from the Hammonds, she came to see her gang members daily. They would gather to hear her latest instructions and to do her bidding, above the grocery store on the corner of the block across the street from where Clem lived. Right after Clem's family moved to Greenwood, the gang members showed an interest in meeting her and walked across the street to talk to her. It was then that Ida Mae appeared from around the corner of the grocery store and, glaring fiercely, came limping over to them. Clem could hear dismay in the whispers of the group and noticed that Ida Mae had fixed her eyes upon her, and her alone, as she came up to the group. Something in those eyes reminded Clem of a lion stalking towards its prey. Politely, the group introduced Clem to Ida Mae and fell back a bit to let the two of them become better acquainted.

There's no doubt that Clem could have handled that meeting with more tact, she thought later. But she was a child, not a skilled speaker, and was very interested in this strange girl who provoked such temerity among her friends. After their introduction, Clem asked, "What happened to your leg?" thinking this was a good place to start a conversation.

Ida Mae exploded into a wrathful and vindictive tirade against Clem, accusing her of feeling "superior" and of being "rude." There was a lot more, but Clem was so taken aback that she almost could not hear properly. Ida Mae concluded that she would never forget such an insult, and that she would get revenge on Clem. As she turned to leave, she spitefully informed Clem that she had had polio, and that's what was "wrong with my leg." Giving Clem a last nasty look, she hobbled away, while the other gang members suggested that Clem should just forget about it, because Ida Mae was always in a bad mood.

As time went by, Clem found out that the gathering place above the grocery store was actually an apartment that the family of one of the gang members lived in. Clem never saw any kind of parental figure there and was informed by the gang only that the mother worked. The apartment was without furniture, not even a table and chairs, but in a room off the main room were several broken-down beds and some rumpled bedding. The rooms were always littered with a variety of food wrappers. Although Clem's father and mother were not well-to-do, neither were they as poverty-stricken as some of their neighbors.

When Ida Mae was due to arrive, the gang members would show up at the apartment and wait for her. If Clem was around, they would tell her to leave before Ida Mae arrived, as Clem's presence would be certain to inflame Ida Mae's wrath. On the few occasions that Clem could hear Ida Mae speaking, it was always in a low growling tone, heavy with threat and cocky with self-assurance. Clem relaxed a bit, knowing that this was just the way Ida Mae talked. There was even a seductive, personal tone to her growling. The gang let it slip that they were given chores to perform for Ida Mae, who, they said, was actually a police informant.

Then, Ida Mae did what she always did. After threatening Clem with all manner of revenge, she suddenly extended the olive branch of friendship. Clem was invited to join the group for their daily get-togethers. But Clem had to prove her worthiness to join the gang. The way Clem would prove her friendship to Ida Mae was to steal something from the grocery store downstairs. Wait a minute, thought Clem. Didn't they tell me that Ida Mae was a police informant? Isn't stealing against the law? Why would she want me to steal something to prove my friendship to her? The gang seemed to be galvanized into action. They took up positions all around the grocery store to make sure Clem didn't try to sneak off with whatever goods she stole. Just where Ida Mae would be, Clem didn't know.

Nervously, she entered the grocery store. A couple of the gang members were talking to the store owner, who was behind the meat counter. They were to keep him occupied and distracted so Clem could accomplish her theft. Staying near the front of the store, Clem looked around for something to steal. Her eyes fastened upon a row of large glass jars with lids, each one containing a different kind of big cookie. They were all just about the right height, on a lower shelf. She backed up to the row of jars and using both hands behind her back, lifted the lid of one jar and removed a cookie. She replaced the lid, shaking with fear. She had been instructed to go next door into the hallway that went upstairs and wait for the gang to join her there.

Alone in the hallway, Clem breathed deeply, trying to calm herself down. She felt oppressed by a sense of guilt over the stolen cookie. Was it really the only way to make friends here? The only way to gain acceptance among her peers? She tried to put the whole event into the larger picture of her life. What exactly did it mean? Would she go to hell? No, she thought. She could always repent, make amends. But that idea made her feel even worse. She thought that what she had done was to place her life into Ida Mae's hands, that Ida Mae would from this time on, own her, body and soul. She would have this hanging over her head for the rest of her life. "Oh God," she moaned, "What can I do?" As if in reply, a voice inside her head said, sensibly, "Eat the cookie!"

And that is what Clem did. She ate that big cookie as fast as she could, shoving it into her mouth, chomping it down, brushing her mouth and face with her hands, brushing her dress down, using her tongue to clear away any crumbs that might be sticking to the inside of her mouth. And not a second too soon; the gang members swirled in from all doors and converged upon her.

"Where is it?" they demanded. "What did you steal?"

"I couldn't," Clem said, shrugging her shoulders, looking as miserable as possible. "I just couldn't do it."

All of them let out an explosive breath of disgust as Ida Mae came through the door. Clem stood there, waiting for judgment from the boss. Ida Mae and the others came very close to her, inspecting her face and clothing very closely. But she had done a good job of getting rid of the evidence.

"Well, that's it, then," said Ida Mae, angrily. "You're out! You're no friend of mine, then!" She shook her fist in Clem's face. "The same thing I said before applies to you. Now I'll get revenge! Go on! Get out of my sight!"

Clem hurried home, feeling just a bit of a glow of success, happy in her heart and mind. That was a close call, she thought.

Chapter 10

Clem's Solution

Over the course of the next few years, Ida Mae never let up on Clementine. She told lies about her that got Clem punished every time. No one seemed to believe when Clem said that Ida Mae was lying. It was uncanny the power she had over most people's minds and wills. And her gang, although looking sympathetic towards Clem's predicament, never spoke out, always backed whatever Ida Mae said. Clem became despondent, dreaded any encounter with Ida Mae, who seemed to be able to slip up behind her and start talking. It always ended up becoming a trap for Clem.

When Clem could stand it no longer, she thought long and hard and, eventually, came up with a strategy for dealing with Ida Mae. It seemed childish to Clem, but she was desperate. Whenever she spotted Ida Mae approaching, she would put aside her natural shyness and start yelling loudly, "Say away from me, Ida Mae! I see you there, sneaking up on me! All you ever do is tell lies and make trouble for me!" And she would continue yelling loudly, until Ida Mae left. Everyone in the area could hear what Clem was shouting very loudly and would stop and stare, first at Clem, then at

Ida Mae. At first, Ida Mae tried to pretend that everything was normal, she even laughed at Clem's silly yelling. But it happened every time she tried to get close enough to start more trouble, and she couldn't make any headway in her efforts. Everybody would draw close, trying to hear what was being said. The kind of things Ida Mae was trying to get away with always needed to be done quietly with a low, threatening tone. Now she couldn't intimidate or challenge Clem while all eyes were upon her. Clem was amazed and gratified that her simple ploy was working. Ida Mae would make a sour face and move away. It seemed to be the end of the persecution, for the time being.

Eventually, when Herman's insurance agency became well established and profitable, he and Phyllis moved to another part of town, to a bigger, better house. Clem went to a different school. She no longer saw Ida Mae, to her great relief. But even though she eventually forgot about Ida Mae, she had not been forgotten. Not by a long shot.

She had not been forgotten by Judge Carmine Williams, who by now knew that all of the children in that Fifth Grade classroom had heard his daughter raging and crying. Ida Mae, his own personal "ward of the court" told him everything. She even told him about Eddie, the boy who always wrote things down in a notebook kept in his shirt pocket.

Ida Mae had become what mother and daughter wanted her to become, the judge's on-demand sex toy. She didn't live with them, but a phone was installed in Ida Mae's house, at the judge's expense, so she was available at any time. It especially galled the judge that Clementine Hammond had successfully evaded his clutches in the darkness of that bedroom. Who was she to flout the will of her betters? She was of the lower classes, the "bourgeois" as he liked to call them. In fact, it was one of his favorite words to describe the townspeople. Ida Mae quickly picked up the word and began to use it in the same manner as the judge.

Jack Mooney, now the chief of police, had not forgotten about Clem, either. Once, long ago, when Ida Mae had used her police whistle to bring him running, it was to insist that Clem had stolen a box of watercolor paints from the store they were all standing in front of. And here was the evidence of that! She triumphantly handed the box of watercolors to Mooney, which the gang had taken away from Clem as she exited the store. The gang had surrounded Clem, who was pale and frightened but still defiant. When Mooney said that they had done a good job catching the thief, Clem produced from her pocket the folded receipt and expected to be exonerated of the charge. Mooney entered the store with the receipt to question the store clerk. The clerk verified that the girl had just purchased the paints and that the receipt was valid.

No one, repeat, no one gets away with that kind of sneaky behavior, thought Mooney. Why hadn't she shown the receipt to Ida Mae? Why make him come running for no good reason? It was all Clementine Hammond's fault! He was so angry that he dragged the girl by her arm across the street to her house and told her mother that she had just been caught stealing a box of watercolors from the store across the street.

"Why?" screamed Phyllis, already smacking her daughter. "Why would you do such a thing, when I gave you money to buy the paints?" Jack smirked to himself as he backed away, the receipt in his pocket now. Just let that fool of a clerk try to stick up for the girl. He had shaken his fist in her face, and she had blanched white as a sheet and seemed about to faint. Returning to Ida Mae and her gang, he patted her on the back and told her, in front of the others, that she had done a good job. The gang members nervously exchanged looks, but no one spoke.

All that had happened years before, and Clem had just about forgotten Ida Mae and her gang, the judge and the police chief. After a few years, she entered high school and saw Ida Mae again, and it brought back memories. But Ida Mae did not approach Clem, and they had few encounters until the fateful night that Eric Alderson was so brutally bludgeoned.

It was as if the years between had not existed. Ida Mae looked exactly like she had looked back in childhood. The same crusty eyes, the same sour smell of poverty, the same limp, the same hair style, the same type of clothing; she was now taller, that was the only difference. And she still controlled the same gang members, who always hung out around the doors of the school after class, apparently engaged in some sort of surveillance activity Ida Mae had directed them to do.

Ida Mae seemed to have made some sort of special arrangements with the high school principal, because she came and went in classes according to her own schedule, always carrying an important-looking folder tightly clutched to her person and never participated in class activities or discussions. At times, she was joined at the back of the classroom by one or more of her gang, where she could sometimes be heard talking behind her hand in her characteristic low growl. Teachers were always polite to her but seemed to ignore her presence. Clem could only wonder if she was there as a student, or if she was there as a police informant, or if she was still involved with Judge Williams.

Chapter 11

A New Threat

Buck stood on the walkway, looking at the girl sitting there in the swing on the porch, in her cute little sundress. He studied her knowingly, as a stalker studies his prey, as the hunter looks over what he intends to kill. The look was deliberately carnal and cruel, very long and slow. It made Clem's blood freeze in her veins, gave her a feeling of such imminent danger as she had never known before. Her rational mind struggled for air, struggled to keep her from running, screaming into the house.

Buck's cousins walked right up to the porch. Some sat on the steps, some lolled near the girl, waiting for his signal. Buck nodded his head slightly. "Hey, what's your name?" began one of them. Clem took a breath, looked at the inquirer, who leered at her, but did not answer.

When she did not reply, Buck tilted his head to one side, and the cousin backed away slightly. "Come here," he said, looking at her, "I want to talk to you about something."

"No," she replied quietly, got up and walked into the house, sure that her knees were visibly shaking. From behind the curtained glass front door, she saw Buck move away casually, carelessly flicking his cigarette butt into the bushes. His cousins followed him back to the car they had come in. Clem felt an unholy fear in the pit of her stomach.

It was a hot summer day, and Clem had taken refuge from the heat on the front porch swing where it was shady and she could catch a breeze, or create a breeze by swinging. The car had pulled up and disgorged five men; the father had come to talk about insurance with Herman and walked right into the house past Clem, asking only if this was the insurance man's office.

It was Jack Mooney's brother who came to inquire about insurance, at the request of Jack himself. And he had sent along his eldest son, Buck, with instructions. "Don't rush. There's no need. You don't even have to speak, just give her the look. There's no need to be involved at all, no need to tip your hand. Control everything from the background. Don't show any emotion, that's a dead giveaway. But never give up, you'll come back another day. Bide your time, keep a cool head."

Some of Buck's cousins were already in his gang, and they liked to call themselves "Buck's Bushwhackers." From an early age, Buck imitated his father's every move. If Jack did something with a hammer, there had to be a toy hammer for Buck to play with, right near his father. So it was no surprise to anyone when Buck began to imitate his father's ways, gang-style, as soon as he got older. Jack began to coach him regarding the treatment of women and prisoners; women who were not complicit and did not obey, and men or boys who were taken as prisoners if they did not cooperate.

Now Jack had given his son a mission to work on Clementine Hammond. Break her loose, get her alone, terrorize her into doing something which would later be called whoring. From then on, she could be coerced into the trade and be controlled by Buck and his gang. That should settle the uppity girl's propensity for disagreeing with Jack's truth, the truth he was still so fervently committed to, which was to maintain that Ida Mae had not been anywhere in the vicinity when Eric Alderson had been bludgeoned. Even though that event had occurred last March, it was by no means resolved.

Jack Mooney had already taken care of two of the witnesses. Chase and Duke Norris had easily been dealt with by clapping his arm around Chase's shoulders, laughing with him over his "lord of the underworld" self-chosen nickname, and signing him up in his little black book for a monthly stipend of no less than $80.00. Chase would maintain, under oath if necessary, that he and his brother had been having sexual intercourse on the street with Clementine Hammond, and that Ida Mae was not there at all. Eighty dollars a month was a lot of money back then, and Chase's eyes shone with fervent resolve. No problem, sir. Just tell me what to say if I have to testify.

His brother, already on probation for slashing someone with his switchblade, was another matter. Chase would be expected to keep his brother from talking, doing whatever was necessary to shut him up. His criminal conduct would be used to prevent him from ever being called to testify. And when he was finished with high school, Duke would be moved to another town outside of Green County. He could come back only to visit his ailing mother.

The monthly stipend would be classified as his father's pension plan, or insurance fund, to explain the money paid to Chase, if anyone ever asked. Chase's father, one of Greenwood's finest, had died several years before. But there was no pension plan, back then, and Chase's father had no life insurance, either.

Clem's account of the night in question had been discredited and filed away as quickly as possible in an obscure location. Of course, there was no need to bother Ida Mae with any of these details. She had already lied to the judge about her "other" night-time activities, and if she knew Chase was being paid $80.00 to lie about Clementine Hammond, she might start wanting to be paid, too. Even though the lying was all being done to protect Ida Mae, you never could tell what she might try to get away with.

Chapter 12

The Scribe's Notebooks

Eddie "the scribe" Dart lay writhing on the ground, twisting from side to side, trying to avoid the worst of the kicks and blows he was receiving. Nearby, in the pale moonlight, Buck stood thoughtfully moving a toothpick from side to side in his mouth, as if timing the beating. Eddie was a tough little nut, Buck thought, not crying out in pain or begging for mercy. In time to prevent Eddie from being beaten unconscious, Buck gave a signal to his gang, and they stepped back. Clarence and B.J. grabbed Eddie's arms and hauled him to his feet. Blood trickled out the side of his mouth. He coughed a few times. Buck reached out and ripped the notebook out of Eddie's shirt pocket. It was a small 3" x 5" spiral-bound, with a stubby pencil attached to the metal spiral with a piece of string.

Holding out the notebook for all to see, Buck thumbed through it and flipped the pages back with his thumb, glancing at the writing that could only be seen dimly in the moonlight. It was about half full of writing.

"Eddie, you little snitch!" Buck sneered. "What the hell do you think you're doing here? Spying on people and keeping track of every little thing they do! You've been doing this for years. Is this all you've got in all this time? I'll bet there's more little books like this one, yes?"

Eddie nodded slightly, shrugging his shoulders. He had been expecting this for years. He had prepared for it by creating duplicate copies of his little notebooks, in case they were ever lost or stolen. Buck and his gang dragged Eddie off into the night, back to Eddie's house, to retrieve those notebooks. Even so, when given over from Eddie's secret hiding place near his house, there were not enough to satisfy Buck. "Where's the rest of them?" he growled.

Eddie shook his head. It was difficult to speak. His jaw felt like it was broken. "There were more, but they got ruined. They were buried in a plastic bag, but the bag had a hole in it. When I dug them up to move them, they were just a gooey mess. I had to throw them away."

Buck's eyes narrowed. "You better be telling me the truth, Eddie. You know what I do with liars, don't you?"

"I'm not lying to you, Buck," said Eddie, as earnestly as he could. "Honest."

Buck clapped his hand on Eddie's shoulder so forcefully that Eddie almost flinched. "Good, good," Buck said, nodding slowly, and giving Eddie a small push, sent him on his way back towards his house. Eddie wondered only what could have taken the powers that be so long to come after him and his notebooks.

It began with an apoplectic phone call from Judge Carmine Williams to the Police Chief Jack Mooney. The judge alternated between raging about his daughter's behavior and ruminating about the possibility of certain things coming to light about his past conduct. Once Jack got it all sorted out in his mind, it turned out that the judge's daughter, Sylvia, had lost the companionship of her lifelong friend, Joan, who had been sent off to attend a private school. Sylvia had immediately replaced her friend with a lesbian lover. Sylvia and her lover flaunted their relationship in front of the judge, their schoolmates and teachers, and anybody in public places. People began to talk and complain about their profligate behavior. The irate judge stormed at Sylvia and Candice and forbade them to see each other again. This provoked a direct and public confrontation between Sylvia and her father. She loudly proclaimed her hatred for him, claiming that he, by sexually molesting her in childhood, had caused her to become a lesbian, and that she was proud of both her hatred for her father and her lesbianism. She threatened to make speeches on the steps of the court house, even outlining a political agenda that she knew would infuriate her father.

Ida Mae had told the judge about Eddie Dart and his note-taking years before. Now in her late teens, she was still the judge's favorite plaything, having learned by now his likes and dislikes. He had not molested his daughter since he had complete access to Ida Mae. Shouldn't that count for something? Of course, he knew nothing about Ida Mae's other activities.

The judge's wife, Carol, remained aloof and oblivious to all this turmoil. She was loyal to her bridge members and her golf game. She often turned out recipes whose aromas wafted through their societal doings, making their luncheons special. Her manicures and hair appointments were sacrosanct. Cut flowers from her garden adorned the hallway table. She chaired the committee that provided magazines for the various waiting rooms at the hospital. Let her husband and daughter tear each other apart like mad dogs. She remained pure and above the fray.

But Judge Williams had not forgotten how it all began, and he still chafed at the thought of that smart-ass Clementine Hammond, and how she had eluded him that night. Knowing from Ida Mae that Eddie Dart had made notes on the whole wretched business that Sylvia had blubbered about in school was what prompted the raving phone call to Chief Mooney. He knew that Mooney could help him get back any written "documentation" about that whole business. And Mooney did know what to do. It was not worthy of his own involvement. It was definitely something his son, Buck, could handle on his own.

Later that night, sitting at the kitchen table, Buck was able to read some of Eddie's notebooks. He was particularly interested in knowing whether any of his activities had been noted by Eddie. Sure enough, there was an incident that involved Buck's efforts at whore-making that Eddie had written about to some extent.

The girl involved was Lola Strickland. She and her younger brother, Ike, had been orphaned the year before, and had been fostered by an old couple who lived near the school in what was, virtually, a high spot in a swamp. The man was blind. They did not have enough money to live on, and the income provided for foster care was $115.00 per month. That just about made life possible, if the kids didn't eat too much.

Buck's father pointed the girl out to him, told him she was choice material for the trade. If she became dependent on Buck, he could manage her, collect the money she made, and give her enough to live on, which she ought to be grateful for. This was called "pimping" in the big city, but such talk was to be considered an insult here. Nobody was allowed to get away with such talk. Here, we think of it as "management." Anyone speaking up about Buck's activities would be beaten up very badly.

Ordinarily, Buck went to school in another district and was several years older than the other students, but his father made all the arrangements for him to live with relatives in the same school district as the girl and her brother and to be placed in the same grade as Lola. That was the same school that Clem and Eddie attended. Little Ike, Lola's young brother, was only five years old and attended kindergarden in the afternoons, while Lola was in sixth grade with Eddie and Clem.

The persecution of Lola began after school was out for the day, as she walked home with her little brother. Buck's gang members joined him after school and they would surround her and talk to her about what they wanted her to do for them. Buck spoke to her during the school day every chance he got, wrote her notes and leered at her constantly. Lola seemed unmoved by his attention, but of course, she was afraid, and her fear deepened when threats against Ike began.

Eddie made notes. Since earliest childhood, he had felt called to be a witness to things that he observed going on around him. It had always bothered him when lies prevailed, and some people were able to get away with almost anything. It was the cruelty, the soul-hurting, people-destroying things that went on regularly in his own community that needed to be witnessed and recorded. His fellow students relied on him to keep accurate records on everything that happened.

Recess time was the worst for Lola. She wanted to stay in the classroom; the teacher forced her to go outside. She tried hiding in the bathroom; someone complained and out she went. She went to the principal to no avail. She must obey the rules like everybody else. Outside, the cat-calling began while she clung to the handrail near the door. The bullying began in earnest. In fact, the teacher and principal, and most of the students had already been cowed; they knew very well that they did not have the courage to stand up to the police chief's son. No one had stood up when Sylvia began her crying and begging, either. It was rough to be an orphan or have whatever weakness the victim exhibited.

Buck stepped up the campaign. Now he got all the other students involved, knowing that the teachers and the principal would not stop him. He got himself a notebook, wrote down the names of all the students in Lola's class, made a "yes" and a "no" column alongside their names. He made sure that all students in that class understood what they were to do. They were to spit on Lola as they exited the school. Buck stood nearby to make a checkmark in each column as they passed her. Eddie would not spit on her and received a check mark in the "no" column, plus a later beating. Clem, who was the last one to exit the school, looked at Lola sorrowfully, but made at least a spitting gesture as she passed her by. Buck cawed derisively, but gave her a check mark in the "yes" column. Each student was thereby tested, and each one had to live with their conscience thereafter. But Lola did not cave in to Buck and his gang.

Buck and the gang set up a date by which time, if Lola did not give them what they wanted, they would kill Ike. The whole school lived in dread and sorrow for the boy, so young, so sturdy and blond, with thick glasses. All the girls loved Ike, and nobody wanted to see him harmed. Some of the girls advised Lola to give in to save her brother. Lola did not give in. She had, by this time, become distant, stoical to the point of not caring, rarely speaking to any of them. Her eyes had a sunken expression.

At a signal from Buck, Ike was attacked one day at the skating rink. His glasses were smashed on the ice nearby. He was kicked numerous times by attackers wearing hockey skates. He was pounded to unconsciousness. All the girls were crying. Eddie Dart held back tears, bit his lip and took notes about who had been in on the attack and what they did to Ike. Then he left quickly to preserve his notes. The attackers were everywhere, skating among the students and onlookers, watching for dissent or objection. Clem's late arrival was noted, and they thought, when the police and an ambulance arrived almost immediately, that her behavior was suspect.

Who had called the police and ambulance? Who dared to defy them? Of course, it was Clem, who had lived in an agony of conscience since she had not had the courage to openly defy Buck at the spitting-on-Lola debacle. But she had not identified herself to the police, had called from a payphone. She stood there crying with the other girls. No official conclusion was reached about who the snitch was.

Ike survived. He was taken to the hospital, and a month later, was back in school, a little sadder, perhaps, but still the same lovable boy. He even had new glasses now. But Lola's defiance would not stand, Buck decided. He and his gang caught her and gang-raped her. Buck cut a deep gash down the side of her face from her eyebrow to her chin. It created an ugly scar that would remain as a constant reminder of what would happen to anyone who defied Buck Mooney. And it wasn't long after that, that charges were filed against Lola for shoplifting, and she was sent away to a reformatory. The judge wrote in his sentencing that Lola seemed to be "incorrigible." Ike was sent to live with another family.

Reading Eddie Dart's notebook about his failed effort at whore-mongering made Buck's neck veins swell up and his head pound with rage. It was his first real failure at controlling others. Just finding all this information in Dart's notes made him hate the scribe even more. He would get him some day for this.

Chapter 13

Eddie's Love

Eddie Dart loved Clementine Hammond. He had always loved her, since he first set eyes on her when her family moved to Greenwood, when she was seven years old. His rapture was so intense that he wrote a poem about his love for her which was never meant to be seen by other eyes. But his older sister, Verna, went through his things one day looking to see if he had written anything about her misdeeds, and came across the poem, folded tightly into a small square. She read it, or mis-read it, and thought he was in love with Nancy, one of Verna's friends. To Eddie's deep chagrin, she read the poem aloud when Nancy came over to the house and everyone whoo-hooed, laughed, made comments, and teased Eddie endlessly. Eddie never revealed who the poem was really about.

Clem never spoke to Eddie while they were in school, though she liked him and wanted to be friends, he always had the knack of turning away just as she was about to speak. There was an incident that Clem wanted to thank Eddie for, when he had intervened on her behalf. A group of rednecks had her up against a stone wall, where they were threatening her because they thought that her having red hair meant she was a witch. They were closing in, just as Eddie and one of his friends passed by, climbing the stairs next to the wall.

"Leave her alone! She's not a witch!" said Eddie, in a very authoritarian tone, intent on climbing the stairs and minding his own business. In unison, the rednecks backed up, staring at Clem wordlessly. If Eddie Dart, the scribe, who knew everything about everybody, said she was not a witch, then she must not be a witch. "Go on! Get out of here, then!" they snarled. "And stay out of our neighborhood!" Clem wanted to thank Eddie, but he was never available. On the last day of school, Clem realized she would not be seeing Eddie again in the foreseeable future. She had never been able to thank him or even speak to him. She waited outside near the school door for him to emerge, and when he did, he was startled to find her there. She leaned forward, hanging onto the railing. "Hi Eddie, how you doing?" she began, smiling.

"Fine, just fine!" he replied. "And that's the last time we'll be speaking to each other," he announced in a stern tone, turning his back and walking away. Clem did not move or even take a breath for several seconds. Looking after him, she could only wonder what was the matter with him.

Eddie cringed every time he thought about the way he had treated Clem, the girl he loved so very much. He was not as rude to strangers as he had been to her. It was the shame and pain of having his feelings exposed and trampled on by his sister, when she held him up to ridicule by reading his poem aloud to others.

It was the last year of high school, and if Eddie was ever to make his move on Clem, it would have to be soon.

The Homecoming dance was nearing. Clem had not been asked, but friends approached with Eddie's question. He was wondering who she was going to the Homecoming dance with, and if she was not going with anyone, would she possibly be interested in going with him. Not that it mattered, of course, he had added. Just curious, that's all. Clem sighed deeply and shook her head softly. What was the matter with Eddie? Why so cautious and round-about? Why didn't he just ask her himself? Wearily, she told the go-betweens that, yes, she would be agreeable to going to the Homecoming dance with Eddie, but only if he asked her himself, person to person.

Eddie showed up at the house that evening after dark and knocked on the door, heart pounding. Clem answered the door, invited him in with a smile and an exaggerated, sweeping gesture and closed the door after him. There, in the soft glow of the foyer, they gazed at each other, Clem waiting with arms crossed, tapping her toe, Eddie intense. It was not long before they were both speaking from the heart. Long-held secrets were told, hands were held, eyes shone like velvet pools, lips brushed against lips, smiles were felt cheek to cheek, sighs and deep breathing, arms intertwined, hugging and leaning closely. Oh, and Homecoming! Yes, they laughed, the dance. Of course, we're going to the dance, just days away. He would pick her up at 7:00.

Chapter 14

Eric's Family

Across town, Eric Alderson had recently returned home after six months of intense medical procedures, psychological care and physical therapy. He felt pretty good. His two young sons were happy to be with him. His wife, Joyce, was another story. Blonde, beautiful and cat-like, Joyce smiled prettily to herself and gave him a simpering pout, meant to be sexy. Eric had recently been told by his best friends that Joyce was perhaps a bit too chummy with the pool boy. The pool had been drained for the winter, and Chad was no longer needed to maintain it, but the teenager was still seen coming and going on a regular basis at the house. Would Eric be up to the task of taming his golden-maned lioness?

His own hair, once flaxen and thick, had disappeared to a mere fringe at the sides and back of his head. He sported a metal plate in the top of his skull and had been advised, with a twinge of humor, to get off the golf course at the first hint of lightning. He would require several more surgeries, each with a decrease in size of plate, before his skull could be permanently grown back together. He could only hope that his hair might grow back, as well.

He had been coached by psychologists very carefully and had come through the trauma in good shape, mentally. He had been able to remember everything that happened the night he was bludgeoned, the night he was pronounced dead on arrival at the hospital. He only needed confirmation of his own traumatic perceptions to assure himself that his memory was functioning properly. He and his father knew who had attacked him. It was the company pilot, Bill Hanson, who had grabbed the poker from the fireplace in the meeting room. Bill Hanson was most likely in the pay of Alderson Enterprises' rival in town, Tom O'Malley. Tom owned a dairy farm and also a restaurant/motel right in the heart of town. Of course, he wanted jet planes to land in Greenwood, good for business, good for everyone. And Bill Hanson was his man, right there to vote for him, even though O'Malley was not at the meeting. Hanson had a bad temper, and when Eric had stubbornly refused to budge on his position, over-riding Hanson's vote, a heated argument broke out that resulted in the attack on Eric. The other members of the council meeting, shocked into silence by the anger exhibited by Hanson, were witnesses to the bludgeoning and had helped Eric to his feet, appalled by his condition.

Eric picked up the phone in his den. He needed to talk to his father. He heard his wife, Joyce, speaking in low tones, telling someone that she would call in a day or two, when it was safe for him to come over. She was on the phone in the bedroom, no doubt. He hung the phone up just as the doorbell rang. It was his mother and father, bringing a casserole supper and a pan of sticky buns. Charles and his son had always been on the same wave length of communication.

Joyce poked her head around the hallway corner, exchanged greetings, and the women went into the kitchen to brew a pot of coffee. Charles sat down with Eric, looking at him keenly.

"How are you feeling?" And when Eric assured him he was doing fine, his father continued, "I wanted to discuss what's to be done about Hanson. We can go several ways. We should insist on a criminal prosecution. Failing that, if we decide not to prosecute publicly, we should terminate his contract, with just cause, and threaten a civil case. We could wipe him out financially, but he is only the bad dog, working for his boss. Do you really want to fly with him at the controls, every again?"

Eric snorted and shook his head, then closed his eyes and nodded. "Whatever you decide to do, dad . . . . I am wondering why the chief of police has been so reluctant to bring charges, do anything, even though we have so many witnesses, including myself."

"I've been thinking about that, too," said Charles, "and one reason may be that you must go to the police and personally identify your attacker. And, I just know it has something to do with that little blonde tramp who was outside the hotel. I think Mooney is protecting her, and slandering the Hammond's daughter, Clementine, claiming that she was the one outside the hotel that evening."

"Do you know who she is?" asked Eric. "The girl outside the hotel? Her face is etched into my memory. I'd be able to identify her easily. Not that it matters, except for Clementine's sake."

For the next couple of nights, Eric drove around town, watching the people who were walking up and down the streets. Sometimes he parked his vehicle in a parking space on the main street, appeared to be reading a newspaper, and kept tabs on who passed by. Eventually, he saw her, the blond girl he had seen leaning against the building that night; now he saw that she dragged one foot, and remembered hearing about her from his mother. She had survived polio, but would always have a stiff leg. He buried his head deep into the paper until she had passed by. He knew she was a prostitute, had heard about her. Probably she was one of Mooney's girls. He shook his head. This town was so riddled with corruption, this small Midwest town. What was it like in the big cities, he wondered; what was it like in politics on the state or national level? He drove home to his cheating wife.

Chapter 15

The Dance Goes On

Phyllis was not doing well. The doctor put her back in the hospital for tests on Friday. Her mother, Maria, was worried. There was talk of removing one of her kidneys, a very serious surgery. Clem held her grandmother and stroked heir hair, but there was not much she could say or do.

Maria had been working on Clem's Homecoming dress. The gown was yellow satin, with a form-fitting bodice, a gathered skirt topped with a wide band of green velvet below the waist, and another band of green velvet that formed an off-the-shoulder neckline. Maria worked on the dress late into the evenings.

Eric and his father had just returned from another confrontation with the chief of police, Jack Mooney. Eric told the chief that he could easily identify Ida Mae March as the girl who was standing near the doorway on the night he was attacked. And he could also say with certainty that he had been attacked inside the building, in the conference room, by Bill Hanson, the company's pilot, and there were any number of witnesses who could testify to the facts. Mooney's face took on a purplish hue, and his breathing became dragon-like. Eric and Charles simply stood there, observing the chief's reaction, glancing at each other as if verifying previous observations.

"Why so upset?" asked Eric, lightly. "After all, if you're just protecting the girl, that's not a problem for you, is it? She wasn't involved in any way in the attack, and neither were the two young men she was with."

This pronouncement seemed to have a calming effect on Mooney, who simply snarled back at them, "It depends on if you two are willing to keep your mouths shut about the witnesses on the street. If you decide to go shooting your mouths off about it, then it could be a problem."

Eric and Charles again exchanged looks. Charles said, "And I suppose protecting the girl was the reason that you refused to accept my affidavit about Clementine Hammond being at choir practice that evening." But this brought back the purple rage and neck-swelling they had observed before. "That girl is nothing but a smart-ass trouble-maker!" yelled Mooney, shaking his fist at Charles. "And as far as I'm concerned, she was there at that time. She gave a statement to that effect. And lied about Ida Mae March being there . . . ." Only then did he realize that his assertion was an obvious bald-faced lie to these two.

"Be that as it may," said Charles, smoothly, "Until 9:00 p.m. that evening, I can and will testify, if necessary, that Clementine Hammond was at the church. What we are interested in achieving here, sir, is a compromise of sorts. We will not bring up the subject of who was outside of the building that evening, but I will not stand by and allow you to impugn the integrity of that girl and say that she was there, doing who knows what with those young men. In return, I want charges brought against the pilot, Bill

Hanson, who attacked my son in that meeting. We have witnesses."

Even after the complaint had been filed and business taken care of, Eric did not believe the police chief had calmed down. Yes, it was always Jack Mooney's way to allow the legal law to proceed without fighting it. But darker forces were at work in his mind, and Eric sensed it. That evening, from home, he called Clem's house. She answered the phone, and Eric asked if he could talk to her in private. He said it was about the night he was attacked, and she agreed to speak to him. Yes, he could come right over. In the bedroom, Joyce quietly hung up the phone she had been listening on.

Clem's father, who was depressed, had begun to stay out late in the evening, sitting in his favorite tavern, drinking. Clem rarely saw him anymore and noticed he was always gloomy and uncommunicative. All this trouble with her own parents increased her sense of abandonment, and tonight was no exception. She wondered if her father even knew she was going to the Homecoming dance. When Eric arrived, it was already getting late, and Clem had been listening to the Homecoming football game on the radio. Eric barely acknowledged the game and asked if she would go for a drive; a short drive, he assured her, so they could talk in private. Once underway, he drove quickly to a secluded area and parked the car. Clem felt uncomfortable and turned to him.

"What is it?" she asked, concerned. "Is there anything I can tell you about the night you were attacked?"

"Well, yes," said Eric, "start at the beginning and tell me everything you can remember. That would help me verify what I have been able to remember with help from my psychologist. It all seems to be like a shifting nightmare to me."

"All right," she replied, and gave him as complete an account as she could, reliving the awful sight of how he looked with his brains sliding out of his broken head. He looked at her with the same look in his eyes as he had that night. And she also told him about Ida Mae March, how she was there, leaning against the far end of the hotel wall, how she looked at him in the car. Eric nodded. He reached out and took Clem's hand in his while he talked about his situation. Clem looked down at his hand on hers, then back to his eyes, questioningly. She knew he was married. What . . . . why? She didn't know what to do and pulled her hand away from his.

Eric drew a sharp breath. What had he been thinking? He had wanted to warn her that she might be in danger, but now he found that he had nothing specific to tell her. It was just a feeling. He leaned back in his seat, staring ahead. Clem looked at the dashboard clock. She needed to get ready for the dance. Eddie was going to pick her up in an hour. Eric started the car and zoomed back to her house in a few minutes. He thanked her for taking the time to speak to him but looked after her for a long time as she made her way inside. If Eric sensed that Clem was in danger, what could he do now to protect her? Eric's father had told him that the police chief's interest in protecting Ida Mae's identity at the hotel that night was that she was the exclusive call girl of Judge Carmine Williams. And the judge did not want his personal call girl to be with other men, as was the case that night.

"You understand that, don't you?" asked Charles. "He doesn't want to risk getting a venereal disease, and perhaps there are other reasons besides. Who knows? He may even be in love with her. But he wants her to be his, exclusively."

The dress was as ready as it would ever be. Clem jumped into the shower and began getting ready for the dance. Eddie, too, was getting ready. He had purchased a small corsage of white orchid for Clem, and a white carnation for his jacket pocket. He had borrowed a car and a suit. Soon, he was standing at Clem's door. Maria ushered him in. Clem was almost ready. Maria was just tucking the last hair strands into a French twist, with a little fan of hair ends sticking up at a clever angle. "Like a fan in your hair," said Maria. The whole arrangement was held in place by invisible forces, as far as the eye could see. Eventually, all three of them, Maria, Clem and Eddie, decided that the orchid should be pinned into the hairdo. It looked right at home there.

"Thank heavens for my grandmother," Clem confided to Eddie. "I don't think I could have survived without her." Eddie nodded and smiled.

Chapter 16

Things in the Works

Jack Mooney's stomach was aching now. Something like ulcers gnawed at his guts. How he hated them, the rich, fat cat businessmen who had such wealth and power. Did they imagine themselves to be better than Jack Mooney's law, the real law of the land? He called Buck to his side for a talk. Buck smiled and nodded, listening to his father, knowing already that Clem and Eddie were dating now, going to the big dance after the game. Mooney growled when he heard that, then he laughed. So the two troublemakers were getting together, teaming up? It was so convenient, it was like having them "packaged" for his son. It would give him satisfaction to know that the two of them would suffer, even if he could do nothing to the Aldersons. Not right now, at least.

All the arrangements were made. Buck's gang was ready to go. They knew that Eddie had borrowed a car. They waited in the parking lot for the grand finale later that night.

Eric yanked open his middle desk drawer and rummaged through things until he found the gun at the back, pulled it out and looked at it. He had gone to his office right after dropping Clem off at her house. He kept the weapon at work now that his boys were into everything at home. He opened a side drawer and rummaged around, found the ammunition. He released the clip and loaded it. He smacked the clip shut. He thought about the steps involved in firing the weapon. Satisfied that he knew what he was doing, he closed the desk drawers, stuck the gun into his waistband, changed his mind and tucked it into his inside breast pocket, which was roomy enough to accept it.

He could not get it out of his mind; that the chief of police would stick to a bald-faced lie about an innocent girl, right in front of eye witnesses who could and would be believed in court. Or should be believed, if sanity had not fled town completely. Eric reasoned that the girl was in danger and knew she would be going to the Homecoming dance later this evening. He knew something else as well; that Joyce, his hot-blooded wife, was going to the Homecoming dance with Chad, their pool boy. What had become of their marriage, he wondered. Was it asking too much of a wife to remain faithful for six months or so, while he was incapacitated? Recovering from a serious injury that still haunted his dreams? Was it the baldness? He rubbed his hand gently over his delicate crown that still suffered ghost pain from his dreadful experience.

But when he arrived at his house, Joyce was snarling and seemed ready to attack him physically, which was her usual way of letting him know he had done something to offend her. He winced, involuntarily, as she came at him, yelling forcefully. She accused him of being unfaithful; she had been listening in on the bedroom phone when he had called Clem earlier in the evening. Now she was insisting that his infidelity was grounds for divorce.

Eric laughed. "No, but by all means, go to the dance with your favorite boyfriend of late. Do you think I'm unaware of what you've been up to while I've been away, recuperating?"

Joyce raged and stormed, threatened, insisting that her attendance at the dance tonight was but a social event that she was expected to attend, to keep up appearances. His not being there could only be explained by his delicate condition right now. It was the least she could do to maintain their expected support of the town's social functioning. Eric left her and went into his den to get an Alka Seltzer and calm himself down. He heard the door slam when she left the house. He laid back in his leather recliner, closed his eyes and fell asleep.

Up on "Knob Hill," Judge Carmine Williams sat at his desk poring over some "documents" under a strong desk light. He grabbed the phone and hastily dialed up Police Chief Jack Mooney. "There's a problem here!" he snapped, when Jack answered. "Those notebooks you got from the Dart boy are duplicates!"

Mooney was silent for several seconds. "How do you know that?" he asked, after shifting gears mentally.

"Because of the writing," explained the judge. "If they were written at different times, as would be expected, the writing would show slight differences for each entry. But these entries are all the same, written at the same time, obviously. I've examined handwriting. You could say I have some expertise at it, and I'm telling you, these are duplicates, not originals!"

"Well," drawled Mooney, "you don't have to worry about it much longer. Things are in the works now that will change the situation. What could I do about it anyway? You want me to haul Dart in for questioning?"

"No . . . . don't know," mumbled the judge, uncertainly. He was looking at the picture of his daughter, Sylvia, staring at him from his desktop. Then he laughed abruptly. What was he getting so excited for, anyway? It was really his daughter who was the problem, wasn't it? "What are you planning to do?" he queried, jokingly. "Oh, forget it! It's not important!" he said with finality, hanging up the phone, chuckling to himself. It was just good to know that the chief was in his pocket if he needed anything. He picked up the phone and called Ida Mae, but there was no answer.

In fact, Ida Mae was doing what she always did, going downtown to take care of business. Nowadays, she used her oldest and tallest gang member, Larry Fisk, to procure customers in bars. He would relay a message to another gang member standing outside near the doorway, who would run to a payphone, call Ida Mae and let her know she had a hot customer waiting and ready to go. Ida Mae lived within three blocks of the downtown area and would soon arrive, walk into the bar. Larry would point out the customer, and she would pass close by the man, growling a few instructions and leave immediately, meeting the customer soon after at a location of her choice. Chief Mooney knew all about her arrangements, approved of them, and as always, offered her his full protection.

At the dance, Eddie and Clem whirled around the dance floor. People smiled at them as they waltzed by. Clem, with her deep red hair and creamy complexion, looked lovely in her yellow satin and dark green velvet dress. Eddie, with his black hair and brown eyes, looked even more handsome in his borrowed black suit, white shirt and iridescent tie. Clem became aware of a strange, hissing sound as she danced with Eddie. Looking around, she saw that every time they came near Joyce Alderson and Chad Evers, the hissing sound commenced and seemed to be coming from Joyce. Yes, it was coming from Joyce, she knew, looking directly at her.

"What was that all about?" asked Eddie, swinging her away to another side of the dance floor. Clem shook her head and told Eddie about Eric Alderson's need to speak to her earlier in the evening about his injury. "He said it would be helpful for his psychological recovery from the bludgeoning if I told him everything I remembered as I passed by the hotel on my way home. Apparently, his wife, Joyce – that was her hissing like a radiator – is jealous about anyone speaking to her husband. At least, that's the only reason I can think of for her strange behavior."

"Where is her husband, then?" asked Eddie. "She's not married to Chad, obviously."

"Who knows? I hadn't seen him since that night. He seemed to be well enough to drive a car or attend a dance, but I don't know where he went after we spoke earlier." Eddie put his cheek on hers and off they went, swirling around the floor.

Chapter 17

The Latest Targets

When Eddie and Clem arrived at the car after the dance, they were quickly surrounded by Buck and his gang. "We have some unfinished business, Eddie," said Buck. "It doesn't concern your girlfriend here, so let's just have her sit in my car while we talk." Grabbing Clem's arm, he took her around to the other side of his car and opened the back seat door. The gang closed in on Eddie, grabbing his arms. Buck pushed Clem roughly into the back seat and closed the door softly while he got something ready from his pocket. "I'll be right there, Eddie," he said cheerfully over the top of the car. "I just want to have a word with your girlfriend, here." Eddie began to struggle, in vain.

He opened the car door and slid in beside Clem, who was doing her best to remain calm. Buck wasted no time. He jabbed the syringe needle into Clem. She felt pain in her side and thought that Buck had hit her with something hard. But a strange sensation, as of deep shock, was already setting in, and she watched, as in a dream, as her hands were bound in front of her with some sort of elastic tie. She had been injected with a powerful animal tranquilizer.

Eddie, still struggling with the gang, could not see what had happened to Clem. Buck returned to Eddie and spoke in a friendly, easy-going manner. "Now Eddie," he began in a soft, scolding tone, "I know you lied to me about those notebooks." As Eddie's hands were tied together behind his back, Buck said, "We are just going to take you over to wherever you have hidden the original notebooks. Once you tell us where they are and we get them, we'll drive both of you back over here. You can be on your way in 15 minutes, no problem, eh boy?"

Eddie was shoved into the front passenger side of the car, and looking back at Clem, he saw that her eyes were glassy and almost closed. She seemed about to slump over. Eddie's heart began to pound harder. "What have you done to her?" he asked Buck, who was climbing into the back seat next to Clem. But Buck just sneered at him. "I'm running the show now, boy!" he snarled. Clarence got into the driver's side and drove off, with the rest of the gang following in another car behind.

They drove to an abandoned farm and quickly unloaded their cargo at the tumble-down barn. The sharp moonlight contrasted starkly with the dark interior of the barn. Gang members lit lanterns as Clem and Eddie were dragged and carried inside. Eddie was tied face down on a bench with his head hanging over a bucket. Clem was carried to an old door that was leaning at an angle against a post. She was placed face up on the slanting door and her hands were tied up to the post. The orchid corsage was crushed and fell to the floor as her hair came undone. Her glassy eyes betrayed no emotion or fear, but very far inside herself, she knew what was going on and realized the danger they were in. Eddie, though silent, was wild with fear for Clem. Her eyes wandered around and fell upon Eddie, looking up at her. She wanted to speak, but couldn't.

Buck grabbed Eddie's hair and lifted his head so he could see the sharp skinning knife he held in his other hand. "Don't worry, Eddie," he said soothingly, "nothing's going to happen to you, at least not yet. We're just going to have a little fun with your girlfriend for awhile. I bet you'd like to watch, wouldn't you?"

Eric awoke from his nap and looked at his watch. It was already 9:30! He jumped to his feet, feeling his breast pocket, and noting that his terrible headache had subsided, he left the house immediately. Getting into his car, he drove quickly to the high school parking lot. He turned off his headlights and backed into a parking space near the exit. From here, he could see the main drive leading out of the lot and away from the school. Not content to wait, he got out of his car and walked to the gymnasium door, peering through the reinforced glass window. Eventually, he spotted her; his wife and his pool boy, sitting at opposite sides of a table. Things were winding down for Joyce and Chad, and they both looked bored, he noted grimly. He could not see Clem anywhere and returned to his car, waiting in the chilly October night.

When the two-car convoy carrying Buck and his gang and Eddie and Clem, left the parking lot, it was an alert and angry Eric who spotted them, crouching low behind the steering wheel of his car so as not to be seen. He knew that Buck was Chief Mooney's son, had heard much about his ugly deeds. He followed them; when they left town, he seemed to turn off, but had only turned off his headlights and kept following them in the moonlight. He hesitated as he pulled into the lane leading up to the abandoned farmhouse, but then he saw them in the pale light, dragging

Eddie and carrying Clem from the parked cars into the barn. He didn't wait much longer. He drove right up to the barn, turning on his headlights and ramming the barn doors with his car, breaking through the old, rotting wood and stopping just inside the door. The startled gang put their hands up to shelter their faces and heads, as Eric jumped out of his car, brandishing his handgun. No one spoke. Eric pointed the weapon first at one man, then the next, to emphasize his readiness to shoot.

"Untie them!" he shouted, as the last splinters from the broken door fell. "You!" pointing the gun. When Eddie was untied, he rushed to Clem's side. She fell to the floor as soon as she was freed. Buck began to speak in a low, menacing tone, promising revenge, but Eric pointed his weapon at Buck's chest and told him to shut up. Eddie picked Clem up and carried her to Eric's car. Eric opened the door one-handed, not taking his eyes or his gun off the gang. When both of them were safely in his car, he edged his way to the driver's side, got in and backed out quickly. As it turned out, none of the gang had thought to bring a firearm with them. Enraged, Buck picked up a pitchfork and hurled it after the departing car. It bounced harmlessly off the trunk and fell to the side.

Eddie stared at the rear view mirror, looking for a return glance from Eric. The two men did not know each other, but Eddie was still speechless. Clem was slumped over on her side, head in Eddie's lap, fragments of bindings still clinging to her wrists. Eric, now back on the highway, looked into the rear view mirror at Eddie and grinned. Eddie nodded, his face twisting half into a smile, half into wanting to cry from relief. "Thank you, man!" was all he could manage to say.

Eric sped back to town, taking Clem and Eddie to his house. There, he called his own doctor for Clem. None of them knew what had been injected into her, and Eric wanted her to have care immediately. A friendship was born that night between Eddie, Eric and Clem that would last many years. Eddie would return the favor someday, he vowed. And Eric needed people he could trust living and working around him. After his traumatic recent experience, he often felt that he was probably surrounded by enemies, secretly nursing a grudge against him. Fighting for the company's interests and his father's ideals had put him into some serious confrontations. He sometimes felt like a gladiator in an arena full of lions and warriors.

Chapter 18

The Aftermath

Clem sat in the hospital room, beside her mother's bed, waiting for Phyllis to wake up, keeping an eye on her breathing. Herman came into the room, looking bleary-eyed and harried, hat askew and tie loosened, shirt unbuttoned at the neck. Clem rose to greet him and hugged him for a long time. He began to cry.

"Dad . . ." she began, but there was so much she wanted to tell him, that she didn't know where to begin. Instead, she focused on the immediate situation. "She got out of ICU about a half hour ago. They said she came through pretty good." Herman took hold of Phyllis's hand and looked at her ashen face. More tears fell. "I got here as soon as I could," was all he could manage to say. They sat in the room together, eventually being joined by Maria, who had gone to the cafeteria for a bite to eat. The time passed slowly.

Clem had awakened after her ordeal at Buck's hands with no apparent problems from the injection of animal tranquilizer, except for bruises and soreness. Eric's doctor had paid a follow-up visit the next morning at her house, to make sure she was all right. Only Maria had been told what had happened, as Herman was not at home the entire evening. Maria only understood that Clem had been saved by Eric Alderson, who instantly was transformed into a hero in her eyes. Now it was Monday, and Phyllis had just come out of surgery to remove one of her kidneys. A very serious surgery indeed, but it was hoped that her health would finally improve now that the bad kidney was gone.

Eric and Eddie had spent the next afternoon together, talking about their town and the syndicate that had been running things to the detriment of the citizens. Eric had offered Eddie employment at Alderson Enterprises as soon as he graduated from high school. He and Eddie talked about his "talent for keeping records" as Eric put it, and the position he offered Eddie would have a substantial income connected to it. Eddie could begin training after school in the afternoons in the Quality Control Department.

Jack Mooney's face went gray as Buck told him what happened after the dance. Furious, and disappointed in his son's constant failure to control either himself or others, he said nothing at first. Buck had brought the entire gang with him in case he needed to verify events the night of the Prom, and he hoped to lessen his father's anger and disappointment in him. It was not until after the gang left the house that Mooney's rage was unleashed. Then the tirade began and didn't let up for a good half hour. Buck put his face in his hands and hoped his father would not beat him too badly. But his father's words were just as bad as a beating.

Yes, that was the way of it, thought Chief Mooney afterward. His best and only protégé was Ida Mae March, the poor, orphaned, crippled girl who had more power and ability in her little finger than big, handsome Buck had in his whole body. Buck did not have what it took to be the boss, even though everything was handed to him. It had been one failure after another. Chief Mooney began to look for another he-man from that day on, a strong-arm who could rule, take over after he retired.

Not all the police in town were Mooney's personal squad. Six or eight men he could rely on were his own death squad, men he had known all his life and who were so deeply involved in his every activity that all his secrets were safe. He paid them well to keep their silence. But none of them would have been able to take over for him. The others would have become jealous and the gang would be broken up by in-fighting. He was looking for someone new. It wouldn't be Buck, unless things changed dramatically.

One of the newer officers on the force was showing promise, and Mooney's only "complaint" was that the officer was honest and given to follow up on every detail, an important trait in police work. Gus Fordham had been hired by Mooney when he first came to town and applied for work at the police department, already an outstanding graduate of law enforcement. Gus had grown up in another, even smaller community west of Greenwood, overshadowed by a small, but rugged mountain range sticking up out of the forest. Officer Fordham was instantly well-liked by almost everyone, but his real talent lay in how he conducted police work. He was truly a servant of the law and the people. He never challenged Mooney's "law of the land" and still got the job done. Oddly, Mooney never challenged Fordham's work, and the two worked side by side with no apparent problems. So far, clashes had been avoided.

But Mooney did not trust Fordham to be his replacement when he retired. He needed someone like himself who would be able to take over and run things and manage his men, who needed to be checked daily for signs of alcohol abuse. He wanted someone hard-working, sober and dedicated to the discipline of maintaining power and control over others. What he needed, he thought grimly, was Ida Mae March in a man's body.

Ida Mae and another, older woman, were currently being employed by Mooney as bus stop workers, keeping the bus station under observation at any and all hours that buses were scheduled to arrive and depart. The bus stop was located on a side street at the rear of a diner which fronted on the main drag. A wide open archway connected the bus station and the restaurant. Ida Mae and her partner would sit in a booth near the archway nursing a cup of coffee and Ida Mae's perpetual notebook, keeping a record of who came and went by bus. The older woman knew everybody in town and if neither woman could identify a person, it was definitely noted and reported. Mooney was kept informed every day of comings and goings in the town. He had older men sitting on benches at the railway station, apparently reading a newspaper, making notes on arrivals and departures. Jack had all these people on his secret payroll, old friends who needed the small income for keeping track of the comings and goings at the stations. It was the way he ran things, and it was the way Ida Mae ran things, too.

When Judge Williams called for his "ward of the court," Ida Mae's "employee" would come running to tell her. This employee also had the task of sitting with Gladys, Ida Mae's grandmother, who was bedridden most of the time. Ida Mae had to think up alibis for her night-time activities, though. It was true, as Charles Alderson had surmised, that the judge did not want to share Ida Mae with other men. As a ward of the court, she was considered to be under the direct supervision of the judge. And he had forbidden her to associate with other men; did not want her going downtown at night, walking the streets. Ida Mae, in her sexiest growl, assured him that he was the only man in her life.

But on one night among many that found the judge at the bar of the country club, he overheard two men, one of them a police officer, talking about a conversation he had heard at the station between Jack Mooney and Eric and Charles Alderson. It concerned testimony given by Clementine Hammond, who had been a witness at Eric Alderson's bludgeoning. Her testimony was that Ida Mae March had also been at the scene, at least in front of the hotel. Jack Mooney was calling the Hammond girl a liar, insisting that the March girl had not been present. The Aldersons did not appear to care whether Ida Mae was present or not. Their only concern had been to press charges against the one they claimed bludgeoned Eric. The judge was intrigued. He asked Jack Mooney for a copy of Clem's testimony, but Jack seemed to have lost it, for now, and could only repeat that Clem Hammond was a liar and a troublemaker. The judge had no trouble agreeing with him on that score.

Chapter 19

Living on the Farm

Eddie Dart married Clementine Hammond the next July, soon after graduation from high school. Eddie's mother and father, Maxine and Ed Sr., had always wanted Eddie to have a dairy farm and hoped that this would be a good time to invest in farm land. They found an old farm that had been abandoned after the surviving widow had died. It was located just south of Green County, where the forest and lake country gave way to broad fields. Early settlers had farmed these fields long ago, but now some of the farms were not as well-kept as they once had been. Ed Sr. and Maxine got the farm for a good price, and wanted Eddie and Clem to move in right away. Ed Sr. began to buy heifers, young calves that would grow up to be good milk producers.

The heifers were moved into fenced acres at the south end of the farm, with access to the barn. But the barn needed extensive repairs, as a huge gaping hole had opened in the middle of the barn roof. But one end of the lower level still seemed safe enough to keep the heifers in during cold or stormy weather, and the well supplied good, fresh water for both the barn and the house. The house was old, and one upstairs window was broken. Were there bats, Clem wondered, or had the owls cleaned out the bats? She would have to find out . . . . she and Eddie moved into the farm house late that fall, and fixed the upstairs window right away.

A month later, she found out that she was pregnant. Eddie had a new car to pay for, and also paid for the farm, the heifers, cattle feed, gas to drive back and forth to his job at Alderson Enterprises, food, electricity, and heating oil to keep the house warm in winter. Yes, there was an old-fashioned oil-burning heater in the living room, which threw all the heat up onto the ceiling and left the lower half of the rooms frigid. They bought much of their furniture at an auction, which they never regretted. But they did not have many furnishings for their home and the house rooms remained mostly empty. The gifts they received at their wedding were a blessing and greatly appreciated.

Clem didn't know a thing about farming, or about milking cows, but she was interested and enthusiastic. She gladly accepted the new responsibility of caring for the heifers. In the meantime, she accompanied Eddie and his father as they visited a neighboring farm to talk about the business of milking cows. Their talk naturally took them to the barn, where the cows were being fed. It was the first time Clem had ever been close to a cow. She had only seen them from a distance, driving past farm fields in a car. She now found herself backed up against the wall, in front of the animals, surprised at how big they were and was horrified when the cow in front of her, safely locked in its stanchion, used its very large, long tongue to clean out its own nose. Eddie covered his face with his hand and turned away so Clem would not see him laughing at the shocked expression on her face.

But soon enough, caring for the heifers in their own paddock became one of Clem's favorite activities. Every day, all winter, she would dress up warmly and head down to the old barn. The heifers could go inside for shelter or stay out in the pasture, as they chose. In severe weather, they would be sheltered inside the barn itself with the door closed. Clem's chores consisted of breaking up bales of hay and tossing the sheaves over the fence to them. Then she would pick up the hose, put it into the large oval stock tank and turn on the water. When the tank was full, she would shut off the water and drain the hose, so water wouldn't freeze inside the hose and break it.

What amazed her was that from the very first day, she could hear the heifers talking to each other and to her, apparently via mental telepathy. Startled by this revelation, she could scarcely believe it, but the heifers were all looking at her, and they knew she was pregnant, expecting a young one. Not only did they know, but they were envious of her condition. Clem returned thoughts to them, assuring them that they would soon be pregnant; in fact, we are all counting on that fact, you know. Nodding to them for assurance, she questioned in her own mind if it was well known that cows are very aware of human activity, thought and language. Cows and humans have been closely associated for thousands of years. We think we know a lot about cows, she mused, but do we ever consider that cows know a lot about us, too?

Maybe it was the long, lonely days of winter that made Clem so sensitive to even the thoughts of animals. Eddie would leave for his commute to Alderson's early in the morning, before it was light out, and return late in the evening, again after dark. Since they didn't have much furniture, Clem had not much housework. The large living room had only a few pieces of furniture convened near the windows. The dining room was empty, as was one bedroom. There was no reason to go upstairs. Maxine and Ed Sr. showed up periodically so Ed could work on the barn roof. Maxine sat in the house with Clem, watching out the window, in case Ed fell or needed help. Clem thought mostly about getting baby clothes and furniture.

Sitting at the front windows, looking out at the wind blowing snow across the broad fields was one of Clem's daily activities. Snow was continually whipped up into strange, ghostly forms that towered over the land and were moved along by the wind. One after another of these specters swirled across Clem's field of view, and the sound of the wind howling around the house and across the landscape became a voice that contained a primitive message. Clem would shake free and make a cup of tea, forcing herself to break away from the eerie sound.

Her greatest personal challenge was learning to build and keep a fire going in the old-fashioned wood-fired cook stove that dominated the kitchen and, of course, learning more about cooking on it. Although she had thought she was capable of putting a meal on the table when needed, she knew nothing about cooking on a wood stove. Her first efforts had resulted in several spectacular failures. There was the fire that was too hot, that blistered the paint on the kitchen walls. There was the fire that would not burn properly at all, smoldering and filling the house with smoke. There was the first bread she made, black as coal on the outside, spurting a volcanic stream of liquid dough when stuck with a knife. But finally, there was success; a pumpkin pie that was good to look at and delicious to eat. The stove also had a 2-burner propane gas cook-top at the side. At least she could fry up eggs and bacon, heat water for tea.

But the fire in the stove was also necessary for heat, so every day, she hoped to sharpen her skills at fire-building.

Clem's pregnancy was coming along nicely. There was no longer any morning sickness, which had plagued her in the beginning. She was healthy and strong. Eddie was making enough money to pay the bills. It seemed that Maxine and Ed Sr. would never sell their house and come to help with the farm, as planned. Clem enjoyed her peaceful life on the farm, learning fire-making skills and cooking on the wood stove, caring for the heifers and sitting at the window, watching the snow devils flying across the land.

Chapter 20

Visitors from the Past

Winter began to lose its icy grip on the land in March, but the wind continued to blow across the broad fields. On this day, the temperature may have been in the warm 20's or 30's. There was no fresh snow to blow around, and all the snow there was, was covered in a glazed crust. Clem slept late and got up around 10:00 in the morning. Yawning, she ran her fingers through her hair, put her feet into slippers and didn't bother to tie her bathrobe closed. She was hugely pregnant and waddled lazily out of the bedroom and into the living room. She went to the window and stared out, blinking, rubbing her eyes. In an instant, she was wide awake, her heart pounding.

Their very long, farm country driveway came from the county trunk road and ran right past the house and down to the barn. On the other side of the driveway was a huge cornfield, which had been fenced off with barbed wire. From behind each wooden fencepost, something unusual could be seen sticking out. One fencepost could not cover a boot, the next fencepost could not cover a scarf that flapped in the wind, another fencepost showed half a shoulder of a coat, and on down the row of posts. Clem's eyes fairly popped out of her head; she could not believe what she was seeing. These clothing items could not have been there alone. People had to be wearing that clothing, and they had to be lying down, one behind each fencepost.

"Oh my God!" screamed Clem. "Are they dead?" She stared in horror and disbelief, her brain trying to comprehend how this could have happened. Surely, people lying out on the ground in this weather would have died of exposure. In a minute, she calmed down somewhat, reasoning that it was beyond all understanding that a dozen or so dead people should be found behind her fenceposts. No, they couldn't be dead. Then she saw an arm move, and part of a hat nodded in return.

But this observation brought on another round of alarm. Who were they, and what were they doing, hiding behind her fenceposts? She had heard no vehicles driving down the long driveway, and could not see any vehicles anywhere. Of course, she had been asleep, and the everlasting wind made so much noise.

Who were they? And what were they doing there? Clem stared sharply out the window at what she could see of them. Well, they weren't the police, or the FBI, for they would have been wearing uniforms. And these clothes were, hmmm . . . . Well, these clothes could be described as odds and ends, or perhaps hand-me-downs. Suddenly, Clem knew who the people were! They were Ida Mae's gang! Ida Mae March and her gang, for reasons unknown, were hiding behind fenceposts in her driveway! But the reason, Clem decided, could not have been a friendly visit. No, this just isn't the way friendly visitors behave. Clem felt a sense of hysteria mounting within her.

And that just wouldn't do. No, Clem did not want her growing baby to feel her stress. She battled to overcome her fears, irrational or real. The best thing to do, she thought, was to take control of the situation as soon as possible. But what could she do? Eddie was at work, 40 miles away, and even though she had a telephone there in the house, the hassle of getting him on the phone and telling him what was wrong, and then the long drive home on greasy winter roads; no, she felt she had to take care of things herself, right here and now.

She hurried into the bedroom and pulled on clothing, quickly tying her hair back in a ponytail. She rushed back to the windows to make sure they were still there, then into the kitchen and put a large kettle of water on the gas burner. Peering into the stove, she stirred up the embers and added a few sticks from the nearby wood rick. Pulling a sweater over her shoulders, she went to the back door of the house that faced the driveway and walked out onto the porch.

"Hey, you guys!" she screamed over the wind. "Come into the house and get warmed up! I'm making hot tea!" Then she retreated back into the house and busied herself, setting out the sugar bowl, cream pitcher, small saucers, cups and spoons, and a box of teabags. But even after these preparations had been laid out on the kitchen table, and the water was beginning to steam in the kettle, there was no response. Clem went to the window and looked out, wondering if they were all a figment of her imagination. No, they were still there, but now signaling back and forth to each other in an animated fashion. Something was obviously holding them back.

Clem went back out onto the porch. "You're gonna freeze your asses off!" she screamed over the wind, hand on hip. "You better get in here, now!" And she went back in, this time laying out a box of soda crackers on a plate, a new jar of pincherry jelly, and stuck a teaspoon in the jelly. They would come in, she decided, or she would go out there and drag them in. And they better not make that necessary, in her condition. Yeah, that's right, she told herself.

They began to straggle in, led by the tall man, Larry. His wife or girlfriend, Clem didn't know which, was right behind him, peering out from behind him and smiling shyly. She nodded to them and pointed to the hot water on the stove, now bubbling away. "Help yourselves," she said, "And there's crackers and jelly, too." Then she left the room, almost giving in to a release of irrationality. She sat on her bed for a few minutes, getting herself together, wondering if she had let her attackers in; then she steeled herself again. She could hear them coming in now by ones and twos; they spoke softly and seemed to be relieved to be out of that awful weather and wind. After awhile, Clem managed to get to her feet and pad out to the living room windows to see if they had all come in. They had not. There was one fencepost that still hid a holdout; someone so tough, so determined to carry out "the plan," that she could not be persuaded to come in. Of course, it was Ida Mae.

As Clem turned from the window, Rita, Larry's wife, smiled from the kitchen doorway and shook her head. "She won't come in." Larry joined Rita, and they both walked up to Clem. "Thank you for your hospitality," said Larry. All of us appreciate this very much, but I have to ask for another favor, besides. We have a rule, and if you can't obey it, then we'll all have to leave and go back out there in the cold."

"What is it?" asked Clem, but she thought she already knew.

"Don't ask us to say what we are doing here, what the plan was" said Larry. "We'd be killed if we told you, so just tell us what the rules of the house are, and we will obey them, if we can."

"The rules of the house?" Clem wondered out loud. She hadn't thought of any rules of the house, but since she was expected to obey their rules, she quickly made up two of her own. "If you use the toilet," she intoned darkly, "flush it! And don't be running up my phone bill with long distance calls."

Larry nodded sagely. "We can live with those rules." But Rita was laughing and ran back into the kitchen, telling the others what the rules of the house were.

The ice was broken. Laughter and smiles prevailed, as the guests warmed up. Soon they were all over the house, talking to Clem and to each other; they were perplexed by the jelly and the spoon, and Clem had to explain how to take a bit of jelly with the spoon and drop it onto the cracker, and it makes a nice little snack to go with the tea. Clem didn't mind at all when they undertook a thorough examination of the entire house and its contents. It was as if they had never been in a normal environment, Clem thought. She was entranced by her guests, and soon, they insisted on going down to the paddock to feed and water the heifers. Clem had seldom had such an enjoyable social encounter, and the whole household seemed to be bathed in a soft glow as dusk fell. The day was fading.

In from the cold, face whitened and pinched by frost, bent over and shivering, came Ida Mae. She took a seat right near the door and refused to drink the cup of hot tea offered to her by Rita. She remained hunched over and stared into the cup, as if reading tea leaves. She had not come in for tea or hospitality; she only needed to warm herself now, or die. Clem watched her silently from the empty dining room, as she felt sympathy and empathy for her old enemy. Suddenly, amazement flooded her senses. Ida Mae was pregnant, even as she herself was pregnant. She couldn't have been as far along as Clem was, and yet she had laid out on the frozen ground in the cold all day long. How could anyone expecting a baby do that and not lose the baby? Her hatred for Clem or her devotion to duty, or both, could be the only reasons. Clem shook her head and turned away. She had realized a change in her visitors as soon as Ida Mae had come in. No more laughter, no more happy glow infused them

As Clem rounded a corner soon after, there was Ida Mae standing in a doorway, and her reaction to seeing Clem was immediate and ugly. She pulled a small knife out of her coat sleeve and, hissing, raised it as if to strike at Clem. Clem was having none of it. She slapped at Ida Mae's arm, knocking it against the door frame. Ida Mae's hand was still cold and stiff, and the knife fell harmlessly to the floor. Emboldened, Clem shook her finger in Ida Mae's face. "If you can't behave yourself like a civilized person, you are going right back out there in the cold!" she admonished. Ida Mae looked shocked and said nothing. Clem retreated, giving her opponent time to recover her senses, if she still had any.

Soon after, Larry approached Clem. "We have to leave, and I think the sooner the better. But I'm afraid I'll have to ask to use your phone to make a call. The only way we can leave is to call someone to come and get us, and it will be long distance." Clem nodded. Larry went to the phone and spoke briefly. By now, Clem's curiosity was burning her up, and she tried to listen, unsuccessfully, to Larry's conversation. After he had hung up, she only looked at him meaningfully, and sadly, too, to think what might have been the outcome if their plans had not fallen through. In a short time, it was completely dark, and a single car came down the long driveway. Clem could see nothing in the headlights' glare, and her guests departed wordlessly, like zombies, now back in the world they had come from.

"Come back any time," she chimed after them. "I really enjoyed today," feeling a little fear returning. Ida Mae turned as she was the last to leave. "Does that invitation apply to me, too?" she asked. "Well, yes, I guess so," said Clem, not very enthusiastically. Ida Mae limped out after her gang. Clem thought she would have quite a story to tell when Eddie got home from work. How could they all fit into one car, she wondered, but she knew they surely would.

Chapter 21

Back to Greenwood

But Eddie was so enraged when he came home from work and heard the story of Clem's visitors that he punched a hole in the living room wall, raving mad and screaming at her. "Why didn't you call me? Just call the front desk and leave a message, at least. What possessed you, not to call?" Clem began to wail. "Eddie!" she cried, "Stop. Please stop it! I didn't want you to be driving on icy roads coming home too fast. And I was able to deal with everything without trouble. I just did everything myself. Don't be angry!"

Eddie's frustration was so intense that tears came to his eyes. His wife, his baby, might have been killed. Who knows what evil plan had been hatched? It was too much to endure without taking action. That's it! He was moving Clementine out of this place, first thing in the morning. While Clem slept that night, he packed up all of their clothing and personal items and put everything in his car. In the wee hours before dawn, he woke Clem and told her to get up, they were leaving. "But where are we going?" asked Clem. "And what about the heifers? Who will take care of them?"

"It's about time my folks took some responsibility for this farm they wanted so badly," said Eddie sternly. "We have the payments to make, I have the driving to do, and you've been doing the work of caring for the animals. Let them drive down here every day and look after the heifers. If they won't or can't do it, I'll hire one of the neighbors to do it, or sell the heifers. They will go fast and bring a good price."

Clem felt her spirits falling to think that she might not ever see her darling heifers again. She felt they were somehow a part of her. Eddie continued, "And we're going to stay at Mom and Dad's for awhile, until I can find out what's going on." Clem made a face at that. "I'd rather stay at my own . . . ." But then she stopped. Both her mom and dad were away, visiting friends in Canada, and Maria had left to visit one of her other children for awhile. And it would be better for Clem to spend the last few weeks of her pregnancy close to the doctor and hospital. She nodded her assent and got ready to leave in the darkness of the early morning.

Jack Mooney's gray face and labored breathing continued for hours as he contemplated his handsome son's inept failure once again to manage even the simplest of tasks. Gas line freeze? He and his cohorts could not manage to start the cars because of gas line freeze? And that was the end of it? He had not been in on the planning of this misguided venture, but he knew about it and knew that his son, Buck, was central to carrying it out. All the plans had been made by Judge Carmine Williams and Ida Mae March. But instead of following through with the plan, whatever it may have been, his son and his numbskull gang had returned to a tavern on the highway about five miles from the Dart's farmhouse after dropping Ida Mae and her gang off at the Dart's driveway entrance. Buck's gang, driving another car, were already inside the tavern, having convinced the barkeep, who lived in an apartment in the back, to open up early this morning, so they could get out of the fierce wind. That fierce wind, funneling down the highway, continued to work on the cars as they all sat inside, drinking and getting their bravado up. Soon they were all pretty drunk and the cars would not start. It was too cold and windy for them to stay outside and work on the cars, so back into the bar they went. The barkeep, guessing they were up to no good, became increasingly uncooperative as they tried to find help in getting the cars running. Soon the gang began to pass out on the floor. That was the end of it. Buck and the gang never showed up, leaving Ida Mae and her gang stranded in the wind and weather.

Jack was concerned about Ida Mae's health. She looked even more drawn and red-eyed as she painfully climbed into the car. Yes, she had instructed Larry to call none other than the chief of police to come and pick them up from Clem's house so far away from Greenwood. She had turned to him for help, not the judge, when the judge's plan had failed. Buck's ineptitude had caused Ida Mae to suffer all day. None of her gang members betrayed any joy or comfort they might have had from Clem's hospitality. Jack felt it was the least Clem could do for them, and allowing Larry to use the phone had finally solved their predicament. Jack left it to Buck to call a tow truck and have their vehicles taken to a garage to thaw. It was hours before the gang was sober and the vehicles able to be driven back to town.

Chapter 22

A Bump in the Night

It was as good a time as any for Ida Mae to tell the judge that she was expecting his child. But was he the father of her baby? She could not be absolutely certain of that, what with her nightly activities that the judge knew nothing about. Still, she was convinced he was the father, and if he was not, she could still convince him that he was. The next morning, she called a cab and took herself to the hospital. She was correct in her presumption that she had pneumonia; she had had pneumonia before, and remembered how it felt. She told the hospital personnel that she was with child, and though they clucked and shook their heads, knowing that she was not married, any attempt to get her to name the father was hopeless. She did call Judge Williams from her hospital room, as soon as she was able, to let him know of her whereabouts.

Jack Mooney, of course, knew she was in the hospital; before he dropped her off at her apartment, she told him she was prone to pneumonia and would likely suffer the consequences of being out in the cold all day. Jack was her first visitor, and she asked him to set one of her girls to watch over her grandmother, Gladys. She knew she could trust Mooney, above all others, to see to every detail. There was a bond between them.

As soon as she was well and discharged from the hospital, she went to see Williams at his discretion. They were alone in the house. Both wife and daughter were gone for the evening. After their lovemaking, Judge Williams laid back in his recliner and lit a cigar, contemplating the ceiling. Ida Mae emerged from the shower and settled down beside him in a smaller chair. She smiled her crooked, cunning, charming smile and cleared her throat. She had to tell him now, before she got any bigger.

"You know, don't you?" she began. He rolled his head to look at her. "Know what?" he asked. But she only coughed slightly, got up and went to a table, leafed through some magazines there, and kept her body in profile to his gaze.

He felt the hair on the back of his neck prickle. "Know what?" he demanded, suddenly staring at her bulging profile.

"If it's going to be a problem for you, I can get rid of it," she suggested, with a wave of her hand. "But as of this moment, you are going to be a father."

"Oh my god!" exclaimed the judge. Then he stopped breathing for perhaps a minute, as if listening intently for some voice, some sound in the ethos to guide him. Only silence met his ears. But Ida Mae had already decided to have the baby. Her pregnancy imbued her with a tremendous sense of power and opportunity, and even love. But would the judge allow her to have the baby, or would he insist on an abortion? It was her strategy to bring up abortion as a possibility, in hopes that he would be appalled and say no, right off. It would not do for Ida Mae to try to push the judge around or threaten him with a paternity suit. He could have her killed. Ida Mae was also counting on the good will of Jack Mooney. She was almost certain that he would support her desire to have the baby, even if Carmine Williams did not.

"Well," said Williams, finally. "Do as you will. It's nothing to me. If a Ward of the Court chooses to have an illegitimate child, that's no concern of mine, personally. No one knows about us . . . ." he lied, paused meaningfully, and continued, "of course, the child could also become a Ward of the Court. We can set it up for you . . ." and he drifted off into speculating about all the possibilities of how the new addition to the community might fare as another peg in his grand scheme of things.

But his mind was racing. There's no doubt that things have changed, he thought, privately. The prickly sensation at the back of his neck had not gone away. He sensed danger and began to wonder just when he had "fathered" this child. Would Ida Mae threaten to expose their relationship? But many men of wealth and power had illegitimate children. The whole thing could be handled quietly. And he sensed that Ida Mae had brought up the possibility of abortion as a "worst case scenario," just to make sure all the cards were on the table. It gave him a lot to think about after she left.

And Ida Mae was thinking, too, at home in the shabby apartment she shared with her grandmother. What was that business about "nobody knows about us?" A lot of people knew about their relationship, not the least of whom was Sylvia, who hated her father and took every opportunity to verbally trash him behind his back. All her gang members knew about it; they were the ones who made sure Judge Williams thought she was always close by, just waiting for his call, while she was busy with other men.

Jack Mooney knew about Ida Mae and Carmine Williams. It was Jack who wanted to place Clementine Hammond at the scene in front of the hotel on the night that Eric Alderson was bludgeoned. He knew exactly what Ida Mae was doing on the street with the Norris brothers. He knew the judge had instructed Ida Mae to stay away from other men. He would move heaven and earth to protect her from the judge's wrath.

Chapter 23

Domestic Bliss and Turmoil

Eddie's sister, Verna, returned from business school two days after Eddie moved Clem into his parents' house, claiming to have "graduated early, with honors." Her assertion met no question or resistance from anyone. There was enmity towards Clem; Verna had long held the belief that Eddie loved her friend, Nancy, and she had never accepted his marriage to Clem. If Eddie was aware of the sniping that went on while he was away at work, he did not show it or appear to know anything about it. Clem was miserable but said nothing.

But one day, Clem overheard her mother-in-law talking on the telephone, her back to the stairway that Clem was descending, carrying a basket of clothing to be washed. She was telling someone that her daughter would never, ever want to be associated with farmers and would never move to the farm they had purchased for Eddie. Mrs. Dart insisted that her place in life was with her daughter and not on some run-down, old farm. Only Eddie's father drove to the farm every day to care for the heifers, and how long would that last? Clem quietly made her way to the basement to do her laundry. Apparently, she thought, Eddie and she were on their own as far as the farm was concerned, and how could Eddie work both at Alderson's and on a farm so far away? How would she, herself, work on the farm and care for a baby? And who would protect all of them, so far away and alone?

Maria knew that Clem would soon give birth and came back from her visiting to be on hand to help Clem, if necessary. Clem was certainly glad to see her dear grandmother again, and took the opportunity to gather up her few belongings and move back home. She called a cab, not waiting for Eddie to come home from work. He joined her that evening, a perplexed look in his eyes. At bedtime, Clem told Eddie what she had overheard and what she had been enduring from Verna's sharp tongue. At first, Eddie was angry about the bad news he didn't want to hear, but soon he calmed down and sat on the edge of Clem's bed, thinking things over in the dark. He realized that Clem had done the right thing for herself and the baby's sake. He was only sad that the farm and the heifers would have to be sold, as quickly as possible. He was gone when Clem awakened the next morning. It was the first good night's sleep she had had since Ida Mae and her gang had paid her a visit.

It was a beautiful morning in spring, sunny and cool, two weeks later when Clem felt the first pangs of labor. She called Eddie at work and soon he arrived to drive her to the hospital. Little Jeremy Andrew Dart was born that afternoon. By now, Eddie had come to a decision about the farm that he and his father had planned many times in the past. The plan was not shared by Verna and his mother, and it would cause a family breakup to continue on that path. Better to put everything on the auction block and give up on farming for now.

Verna dated Chase Norris, and it was a serious, whirlwind romance. From the first, they seemed to be on the same wave-length. They married only two months later, in time to take advantage of the sale of property that Chase had his eye on. It was a small tavern, just outside of town, with a small house trailer on the property. In no time at all, they were making plans for a future restaurant and going ahead full bore, purchasing additional property next to the tavern to build the restaurant on. Chase had always dreamed of owning his own tavern and sat quietly by while his new wife did all the bargaining at every business deal. Verna was a determined business woman who would let nothing stand in her way. Soon, a large diamond ring appeared on Verna's hand to signify her recent marriage, although Chase was still unemployed. Verna knew how to get things done.

Then, as luck would have it, Chase received his draft notice in the mail. It was off to the army for him, leaving Verna to carry on with their plans for the tavern and restaurant. The Korean Conflict, as it was called, was still ongoing, and Chase would be gone until his service was finished. Verna ended up tending bar and dealing with the numerous problems she had only recently thought would be Chase's. She constantly needed help from her mother and father, who didn't want her to be alone while tending bar.

It wasn't long before Jack Mooney, the Chief of Police, came to see her. Assessing her personality and determination, Jack decided she was not one to quibble over legal technicalities. She would do well at any cost, step on anyone's head if they got in her way. She immediately became Jack's customer for all the goods and services he was able to procure for her. Jack Mooney was pleased with

Verna, so unlike that troublemaking brother of hers and his troublemaking wife.

It was Verna's driving ambition to become rich. There was no opportunity lost when it came to making money come her way and preventing money from leaving her grasp. Soon, she had a burning question for Chase the next time he called. She had gotten his bank statement and couldn't help but notice a deposit that came every month, from an unknown source, in the amount of $80.00. He was calling from Tokyo, where he was on leave and was unprepared for her interrogation.

"Where does this $80.00 come from?" she wanted to know.

"Huh? I can't hear you. Must be a bad connection."

"Cut the crap. You can hear me just fine. Where's the money coming from?"

"I can't talk about it, really!"

"Bullshit! We're married. I want to know."

"It's a secret. I promised not to tell."

If Chase hadn't been thousands of miles away, Verna would have pinned him down, but she couldn't get her hands on him, just yet. After much wrangling, he promised to tell her when he returned home from service.

Eddie would never think of leaving his position at Alderson Enterprises. His loyalty to his job and to Eric was paramount, and he and Eric became close friends and confidantes. After his terrible experience with the company pilot, Eric felt he needed employees he could trust, who wouldn't stab him in the back, or worse. It wasn't just physical assault or jealous gossip he worried about. He also had professional enemies out to steal company secrets, and loyal employees like Eddie Dart were critical to his continued success.

Now it came as no surprise to Clem, or Eddie's parents, when Eddie regretfully decided that this was not the time to undertake a farming venture. Both he and Clem thought the idea a good one and wanted to try again, perhaps closer to Eddie's work at Alderson's. An auction was held as quickly as possible, the heifers were sold at a profit, and even the repaired barn brought the price of the farm up and made a small profit, which Eddie gave to his father. The profit from the sale of the heifers belonged to Clem, they all agreed. After all the bills were paid off, Clem and Eddie found a house and some property a little way out of town. It was nicely wooded, with a large grassy field and a small stream in a low spot that flowed away from a swamp that no doubt held a spring deep in its center. Clem felt that perhaps, water would thereby be available to water a garden, at least. She and Eddie were happy at home with baby Jerry, looking forward to the future.

Later that same year, Ricky Allen March was born to Ida Mae. Shortly after she came home with Ricky, her grandmother, Gladys, died. Gladys could not see at all, having gone completely blind by now, but she smiled happily as she caressed her great-grandson's head, and her smile lasted until she passed away. Ida Mae was now the only surviving member of her family, and this made her cherish her son even more. She knew that Clem and Eddie were parents, too, and that they had moved close to town when their farming venture had failed. A plan began to form in Ida Mae's mind, and when it blossomed, she told the judge about it. He listened, mildly interested, fearing another failure. He had been upbraided for the first time ever, by Jack Mooney, for the ridiculous plan to attack Clementine Dart at her farm home last winter. From now on, he and Ida Mae would not depend on Buck Mooney to carry out any plans. Buck and his cronies had stupidly talked out loud about their plans at the tavern, and the recriminations from that county judge were just now being settled. But as he listened to Ida Mae's plan, he realized that a softer, subtler hand might be better than physical assault. Yes, get Clementine and Eddie Dart into legal trouble, instead. Just wait for the perfect opportunity, and let nature take its course.

Chapter 24

A Trap for a Dart

Every three months, Eric and Eddie, along with other employees, attended a quarterly business conference in the southern part of the state. Leaving on Friday afternoon, they were due to return late on Saturday. So it was that Clem was home alone with baby Jerry, on a cold winter night, when a car pulled up into the driveway. It had not snowed for some time, and the roads were plowed and easily traveled. But Clem wondered who in the world could be coming to see her so late in the evening. She snapped on the outdoor light and peered out of the kitchen window, but did not recognize the car parked there in the driveway. She saw two women in the car and wondered if they were lost or having car trouble. As they approached the door, Clem recognized that Ida Mae March was one of the women, and the other woman appeared to be carrying a baby, wrapped in a blanket. Clem ruefully remembered her remark to Ida Mae that she would be welcome to return for a visit. Tentatively, she opened the door and peered out at the two women.

Sure enough, Ida Mae brought up the promise of a welcome if she wanted to visit her again, and Clem reluctantly, but full of curiosity, opened the door and invited them in, the old adage about curiosity killing the cat prominent in her mind. She seated the women at the kitchen table and offered them coffee, or tea, whichever they preferred. While preparing coffee and setting out cups, Clem's attention was drawn to the woman with the baby. The baby appeared to be close to the size of a newborn, and Clem thought that she would have sheltered the baby in another quilt, at least. Was the baby wearing a hat? She was not able to see.

The woman did not speak or even look at Clem. She kept her eyes averted, only looking down at the baby in the blanket, rocking it from side to side, sometimes moving her hand up to the baby's face, adjusting the blanket around the baby's head. Clem stared at the woman; she looked so familiar, but Clem could not place her. She had a long scar running down one side of her face that had pulled her features slightly out of alignment. Could it be? What was her name? Lola Strickland . . . . a shiver of apprehension ran down Clem's spine to think what that poor girl had suffered at the hands of Buck Mooney and his gang. She had not seen her since that time so long ago, but still felt pangs of remorse that she had not had the courage to stand up to Buck and not spit at Lola as she passed. But what could be the purpose of this visit? Was this Lola's baby, or was this Ida Mae's baby? Lola's face had an unhealthy look of grief and pain, and she seemed to be nursing a few bruises; perhaps she was ill. She recalled that it was Lola who was driving the car, and the baby must have been in Ida Mae's lap or on the seat between them.

All this time, Ida Mae had been relishing Clem's obvious discomfort and dismay over seeing Lola again. Now she began speaking in her most effective, insinuating growl, her face cracking into a thin smile. Her voice was so low and soft that Clem did not even hear what she was saying when she first began speaking, her attention being focused on Lola and the baby.

"Was it hospitality, or was it curiosity, that invited us in?" she began, nodding wisely. "I knew I would not be welcomed here, without some sort of lure. But let's see now, if you are as hospitable and charitable as you like to portray yourself to be."

Clem turned her attention to Ida Mae, who now coughed gently and smirked into her coffee cup. "And what does bring you out here in the country this cold winter night?" Clem asked.

"Well, there's time, and time enough to bring up the business at hand. We'll get right to it, then, since you are obviously in a hurry to get rid of us." And here, Ida Mae launched into a long and low-toned critique of Clementine, starting with her lack of courage to even be associated with the likes of Ida Mae and her gang, when she ate the cookie, avoiding Ida Mae's trap. Here she paused to snort her disgust and contempt for Clem, and emphasize that she knew Clem had stolen nothing but a cookie! Then she proceeded to ridicule Clem for her preference for a bath and clean clothes, when she chose avoidance over acceptance of her "station in life." She termed Clem's choices in life as "bourgeois," a word that struck a cord in Clem's memory as a word Judge Williams would use.

All the time that Ida Mae was growling her dislike for Clem and refusing to acknowledge her hospitality or her good will, Clem focused almost entirely on the baby being held by Lola. Its body, within the confines of the thin blanket, was rigid, not curled slightly, as she herself had experienced when holding her own sleeping baby. The baby never moved or made a sound, seemed wooden, even though Lola kept fussing over it and rocking it. And leaning forward to refresh Lola's coffee, which remained untouched by either woman, Clem peered intently at the baby's face and saw that it was gray! Clem began to think that the baby was either dead or dying. A shudder ran through her, and she immediately suspected both women of foul play. But what else could she expect from the likes of Ida Mae? It was apparent that she was not here in the name of friendship.

Seeing the look of alarm spreading across Clem's face, Ida Mae knew that the time had come to get to the point of the visit. She immediately proposed that Clem could reverse Ida Mae's opinion of her by showing real love, hospitality and concern for others. She could take this baby right now, put it into bed with her own baby, and shower it with all the love and care that she was capable of. She could raise this child as her own. No one would ever give her any trouble about the baby, Ida Mae assured her; this baby was Clem's to accept without any legal difficulties at all. Here was a poor child who needed Clem's loving care. And now, would she open her heart to this child, take it as her own, and raise it with the love and righteousness that she seemed to possess? Or was all of that just an empty show?

Clem, who had backed up suddenly, drew a deep breath, eyes wide with understanding. "No one goes around handing out babies!" she retorted sharply. "There are procedures about that, and you, of all people, know that perfectly well. You are no friend to me and never have been, and why would you come out here to "give" me a baby? And I'll tell you another thing," she was shouting by now. "I would never put that baby into bed with my own baby! Who knows if that baby is sick or not? Take that baby, right now, take that baby to the hospital, and do the right thing for once in your life!"

Ida Mae was already rising from the table, and a nod to Lola had her rising too, heading for the door. Neither of them had taken off their coats when they came in and sat down at the table. "Just as I thought!" snorted Ida Mae, as they passed out of the house. "You are a sham, bogus; everything about you is artificial and phony! You don't care at all what happens to this baby."

"Get out!" shouted Clem, as she slammed the door behind them. She watched out the kitchen window to make sure they were really leaving. When they were gone, she locked all the doors, filled a big pan with hot, sudsy water and began to wash everything in the kitchen. The table, the chairs, the legs of the table and chairs, the kitchen floor, the stove, countertops, the coffee pot and all the cups, spoons; anything that had been near the two women was scoured. Then on to the doors, the doorknobs and the floor all the way out the door. By the time she was done scrubbing, her temper had cooled, but the memory of what the baby had looked like still made her shudder. Only after she had thrown all her clothes into the washing machine and taken a shower did she enter little Jerry's nursery and stood looking at him thoughtfully. A tender kiss to her son's cheek and Clem spent most of the night in the darkened living room, on watch all night long.

The baby was Lola's, stillborn after she had been beaten up by Buck. She had refused to have an abortion that he insisted on; whores didn't need to have kids, Buck said. She had stayed with and been kept hidden by Ida Mae until nearly time to deliver, but Buck had found her. After the beating, Lola had given birth on the floor of Ida Mae's apartment. The baby had been dead for awhile when Ida

Mae decided to use it to get Clem into legal trouble. The plan was to have Lola put her baby into bed with Clem's baby, or into Clem's arms before she had a chance to see it, and leave quickly. Once they had left the house without the baby, it would be Clem's problem. From that moment on, they would claim that the baby had been in Clem's care and that she had presided over its death, whatever the cause. The judge could have added lots of charges to the case; he was good at legalese. Clem might even have been charged with murder. Ah, but the bitch was too scared to even pick up a baby. Too bad!

Chapter 25

Verna's Quest

Ida Mae's report to Judge Williams was met with stony silence. Yet another failure? What was going on here? He had obtained the missing police report of Clementine Hammond's interrogation. He had asked the officer whom he had overheard at the country club to get him that report, as a matter of interest in the case involving Eric Alderson v. Bill Hanson, company pilot. The officer told him how difficult it was to locate the missing report; it had been misfiled. He tried to picture the Norris brothers with Clem, who was now Chase's sister-in-law, then put Ida Mae in place of Clem. Which scenario made more sense to him? He pushed the possibility of Ida Mae's infidelity to one side, but the suspicion began to assume a probability that became his constant thought. Jack had assured him that Ida Mae was not there that evening, that it was Clem who had been having sexual relations with Chase and Duke Norris. He would get Chase in here right now, Mooney told him, and the judge could ask him personally who he had been with that night. Carmine Williams felt a sense of relief in the police chief's assertions. It would have been the height of ingratitude and betrayal for Ida Mae to disobey his order to stay off the streets at night and not have sexual relations with any other men.

Time passed, another year went by, and Chase came home to stay, his military service over. Clem and Eddie were invited to a family gathering to celebrate Chase's homecoming. After the meal, when the women were busy with dishes in the kitchen, Chase pulled Eddie aside. "I need advice," he began and proceeded to ask Eddie how to control Verna's strong drive to manage and control everything. "I'm afraid to go to sleep at night. She's jealous of my old girlfriends, and threatens to stab me while I'm in bed. She questions me all the time, she's interrogating me, then she gets a butcher knife and threatens to cut off my . . . ."

Eddie laughed. "She won't do anything to you! At least I'm pretty sure she won't."

But Chase wasn't convinced. "She has to know everything! There isn't anything I own, anything I've ever done, that she isn't into, trying to make something incriminating out of it." Chase was not telling Eddie everything he was worried about. Verna was relentless in her quest to find out where Chase was getting the stipend from, the $80.00 that was deposited every month to his account. He had already lied, said it came from insurance his father carried when he was a policeman, but Verna wanted to call the chief of police and ask questions about the policy. She wanted to know the name of the insurance company and why Chase was getting monthly benefits. Chase threatened to pull the phone cord out of the wall, insisting that she shouldn't bother the chief about that; that he probably knew nothing about the policy.

It wasn't enough to quench the fires of curiosity that burned within Verna. She was relentless. If Chase wouldn't tell her what she wanted to know, she would get Duke and his wife on the phone, ask them if they were getting a monthly stipend from an insurance company, and by the way, what was the name of that company? They wouldn't have known what she was talking about. Chase was forced to insist that he was the only beneficiary. But insurance companies don't do business that way, and Verna knew he was lying. The money had to be coming from another source.

Eventually, Chase gave in and told Verna the truth, or most of the truth, about the money. That he was getting this monthly stipend to maintain, under oath if necessary, that he and his brother Duke had been with Clementine Hammond the night that Eric Alderson had been attacked in the hotel. And that Ida Mae March was not there that night, with them, as Clem had insisted. And Duke knew nothing about it. Because of his past criminal history, he would never have to testify. It all had something to do with Ida Mae, but he wasn't sure what the reason was. Chase hoped that his hasty explanation would be the end of the constant interrogation, but it wasn't.

Verna immediately suggested that $80.00 was too little money to maintain a lie of that significance and insisted that Chase demand more money to keep up the story, especially in the event he would be called upon to perjure himself in court. She wanted Chase to call up the chief of police right now and demand more money. Chase was horrified. He had faced the possibility of combat in Korea, freezing his ass off in a tent, whores out to roll you for everything they could take, seasickness on the way there and back again, but never had he endured such relentless interrogations and threats. He tried to lay down the law, told her to stop, just stop, and be satisfied with what they had.

Verna waited a few days, fomenting her next assault. She reasoned that she couldn't approach the police chief on her own. Her threats to expose the lie would be considered hearsay in a court of law, and she didn't want to arouse the chief's anger. So that door was closed. There was no point in getting Duke involved. He might decide he wanted some of that money too, to keep quiet. And of course, Clem, her despised sister-in-law, probably knew nothing about it. After all, she was the object of the lies that were to be maintained. What to do, what to do. Of course! She could call up Ida Mae and get Ida Mae to help her! Together, they could both clamor for more money. She wondered how much Ida Mae was getting for her silence. Maybe Ida Mae had a few ideas of her own on how to up the ante and put the squeeze on Jack Mooney.

After the phone call from Verna, Ida Mae sat in the darkness of her dingy apartment, shocked at the dizzying array of questions she had mostly avoided answering. But one thing was clear, there was money involved, and it could be a substantial amount of money. It would be something if Ida Mae no longer had to work so hard for what she got. Of course, Verna really had no idea what she was talking about; that had been apparent all through the conversation.

She was angered that Mooney was paying Chase $80.00 a month for his silence, and he didn't have to do anything for the money. Why was he the only one being paid? Why wouldn't Jack Mooney, of all people, pay Ida Mae for her silence? True, she was paid for various jobs she did around town; most notably, the bus station surveillance, but that was a paltry sum compared to what Chase was getting for not doing anything! Maybe Verna was lying about the amount, but there wasn't any indication of that in her voice. And why would she lie about it? Verna's interest had been to team up with Ida Mae to force the police chief to pay more.

Still not satisfied with Ida Mae's reluctance to open up to her inquiries, Verna could only gnash her teeth and wonder what else she could do. What rock could she overturn now and peer beneath?

Chapter 26

Ida Mae Shoots the Moon

In his heart, Carmine Williams knew that Ida Mae was not faithful to him. He had known for years, or at least suspected. Jack Mooney and he had often laughed and joked, "Once a whore, always a whore." Not in regard to Ida Mae, though. The fact was that he needed her, loved her and had come to depend on the relationship he had with her. The other women in his life had rejected him, failed him miserably. His wife, a wife in name only, and his daughter, full of vitriol and spite, made life at home nearly unbearable.

But Ida Mae, with her sour smell that reminded him of some private joy in the distant past, her twisted smile, her sexy, insinuating growl, and her absolute assurance in the face of impending doom that poverty had always inflicted upon him; well, he needed her more than he needed anybody. The child she had borne actually looked like him, even though he had doubts about his paternity. Baby Ricky looked a lot like his mother, he told himself, but he couldn't resist a paternalistic feeling when it came to the child.

On this wintry night in late February, he pulled up to the corner of the block she lived on, and she climbed into his car; a car so tastefully rich, so well appointed, so quietly embellished with everything needed for a romantic encounter leading to sexual ecstasy. There was pulsating music, a tape recorder so he could relive the sound of his mistress's voice, the things she said, the moments of passion he felt. The seat folded back, creating a near full-sized bed. He had everything to ensure a comfortable experience. He sped off, intent on his favorite parking spot, about five miles into the countryside on a little-traveled dirt road off a county trunk road, that the judge himself made sure was kept plowed in winter.

Once in the secluded parking spot, Williams absent-mindedly pushed a button, intending to start some music, but the tape recorder went on instead, he saw. No matter, he thought. Ida Mae looked at the array of glowing lights. She did not know how to run any of the gadgetry on the dashboard, had never learned to drive a car, for that matter. How could she pass a driving test, with one bum leg? She had fortified herself with a shot of peppermint schnapps earlier that evening, before the judge picked her up.

"And what have you been up to, since last we saw each other?" asked Williams, indulgently, as if it mattered. He swung his right arm over the seat and around her shoulder. "Here, take off your coat." He pulled the coat back from her frail shoulders so he could massage her neck and back. Ida Mae smiled at him as he began to gently rub her.

"Not much . . . just the usual . . . you know . . . Ricky needs me to be with him all the time, now" she purred. "I found out something last night, though, something that really has me bothered, and I was wondering if you could help me on this."

"What could it be?" asked the judge, mildly interested.

"I found out that Chase Norris is getting $80.00 a month to tell a lie," she said. "He is supposed to say that he and his brother were with Clem Hammond the night Eric Alderson got his brains knocked out." She paused and turned toward him, suddenly bold. "Jack Mooney is paying him $80.00 a month!" she said loudly, "and my question is, why am I not being paid for my silence? I was there! I saw the same thing that he saw! Why am I not being paid?"

Poor Ida Mae . . . she had completely missed the boat on this one. Either she had not known, or had completely forgotten, in her lust for money, that she was not supposed to be there at all. Jack was paying Chase to lie to protect her from the judge's wrath, and calling Clem a liar to protect Ida Mae from being found out. But no one had ever told Ida Mae to be quiet about her whereabouts that night. Her silence had been taken for granted.

Judge Williams' eyes glowed red. So Jack Mooney, the one person he thought he could trust, the police chief that was supposedly in his pocket, even he was lying to him all the time. And even though he suspected Ida Mae of faithlessness, would she now flaunt it in his face for a price? Would she demand money from him so he himself wouldn't find out about her whoring around on him?

"Are you out of your mind?" he snarled. His hands closed around her throat. "You! . . . . lying! . . . . cheating! . . . . money-grubbing . . . . whore!" With every word, he shook her back and forth violently, as his fingers dug into her throat. He did not stop choking her until, even in his madness, he saw quite plainly that she was dead. Her eyes and tongue bulged out at him from her face. He gasped, tore open the door and nearly fell out of the car. He inhaled deeply in the bitter cold and nearly lost consciousness in the choking that followed. He began to sob. He hadn't meant to kill her. His mind struggled to comprehend the betrayal that led to this.

But, what should he do now? His whole life, his career, was it all to be lost because he was surrounded by traitors? His eyelids had begun to stick together from his freezing tears. He forced himself to get back into the car, while he pondered what to do. Well, Jack Mooney would just have to make amends for his part in this unfortunate event. Jack's betrayal had caused this; Jack owed him, now more than ever.

Chapter 27

The Cover Story

The clock radio on the bedside table woke Clem up at 7:00 a.m. as usual. There was always a blast of annunciatory music followed by the local news. This morning's news was of the tragic discovery of a young woman's body by the side of a country road. The woman had already been identified as Ida Mae March, just shy of her 23rd year of life, the mother of a small child. The death was being investigated as a homicide.

Clem lay there, staring at the ceiling. Eddie, already up and halfway dressed, leaned in on the doorway, staring at Clem. There was not much to say. They got ready to go to work; Eddie as a Quality Control Engineer at Alderson Enterprises, and Clem as a Stenographer/Receptionist, also at Alderson Enterprises. Maria, spry as ever, had come to live with them and take care of their son, Jerry, while they were away at work.

Clem seated herself at her desk in the lobby, riffled through the papers lying there, her mind not ready to begin a normal day's routine typing. Everyone who came through the door must have the same thing on their mind, she thought, though no one spoke of the murder. Not even Eric Alderson, who charged through the door, intent on an upcoming meeting, at which he must play the gladiator again and defend company policy. He was being trailed by two aides, who were focused on the sound of his voice, giving them last minute instructions. Clem thought that she might be feeling a bit melodramatic, thinking and wondering exclusively about Ida Mae, while the whole world continued to spin around, as usual. She sighed and shook her head, focused on her typing.

About 8:30 a.m. though, the door opened and several policemen came into the lobby. The one in front was Jack Mooney, Chief of Police, and he stood in front of Clem, glaring at her while his men moved around the room, checking things out. Clem could only hear his voice echoing in her memory, "If anything ever happens to that poor girl as a result of your lies, I'm going to hold you personally responsible." Clem could barely manage to breathe, as she contemplated being charged with Ida Mae's murder. But they were not here to arrest her. To her utter amazement, Jack Mooney arrested Eric Alderson, had him handcuffed, and he was led out to the squad car, to be booked for the murder. Eric seemed to think the whole thing was a big joke. Laughing over his shoulder as he was guided into the squad car, he called out to Clem. "Call my father, tell him what's happened, he needs to get into that meeting!"

Fairly pop-eyed, Clem called Eric's father, and within minutes, Charles came flying into the lobby. He asked Clem to repeat what had happened to his son, shook his head, and began to pace the floor. "I can't do this for him," he said. "He's the only one who can prevail. Do you know that he is the champion of this company? I'm retired now, and I don't know all the details. I've got to get him out of jail." He snapped his fingers and whirled around. "I know what to do! Call my chauffeur! I'm going down to the police station and confess to the murder myself. They will have to release him!"

Clem called the chauffeur, and the men disappeared out the door. Clem could only shake her head in wonder. Ten minutes later, Eric came flying through the door, still laughing. "They've got my dad . . . just for a short time . . . and now to that meeting!" And he flew down the hallway to another gladiator event.

Clem didn't have long to wait. Eric's father was soon released; his attorney had been called, and the police knew very well that they did not have the real murderer in custody at all. The whole thing had been a distraction to muddy the waters and buy time.

And why did they need to go through that charade? When the judge had returned to town in the wee hours before dawn, he had driven first to the police station, around the back, inside a garage where squad cars were kept. He was met by an employee there, who took care of cleanups of squad cars, both the interiors and the exteriors.

"There's been something of an accident in the front seat, you know the kind I mean," he said gruffly, not looking at the man. "Clean it up for me, will you? I'll see you get paid extra for it." The man nodded. He knew the kind of "accidents" that commonly occurred in the back seats of squad cars from picking up drunks. This mess was quite different, not just the usual vomit. Here were signs of a struggle, scuff marks on the dashboard, claw marks on the arm rest of the door, even a broken fingernail or two. A light glowed on the dashboard. Thinking it was a radio that had been left on, he tentatively pushed a button to turn it off. Out popped an audio tape. Chase pulled the cassette out of the recorder. He put it inside his jacket. Then he went to work, cleaning up the interior.

In the days and weeks following the discovery of Ida Mae's body, there were many news items in the papers and on the radio, sometimes giving details of what had happened to her. Whoever murdered her had attempted to dig a grave to bury the body, probably using a snow shovel kept in the trunk in case of getting stuck in the snow. But the ground was frozen, and the killer had not been able to dig very deeply at all. An attempt to get Ida Mae to fit into such a shallow grave had necessitated the smashing of her skull, still using the back of the snow shovel. Then the whole area was covered with surrounding snow in an effort to hide her corpse. It hadn't succeeded very well. Someone walking their dog had stumbled upon the grisly scene, and the dog had partially uncovered the corpse.

Jack Mooney had listened to Carmine Williams' account of what transpired that night, and the judge's assertion that the chief himself was partly to blame, because he had lied to the judge about Ida Mae's activities. Later, when the judge remembered the tape in the recorder and found it missing, he knew that it would never be returned to him. Jack Mooney had found his new and best apprentice in the "lord of the underworld," one of his own men's sons, Chase had found a way to capitalize on the knowledge of what had happened to Ida Mae. He would not be paid anymore by Jack Mooney. No, now he would be paid, and a lot more, by Judge William, to keep the secret of Ida Mae's killer. Verna would be happy to be getting more money and he just might be getting a good night's sleep at home in his own bed.